I0723040

The Way I See It

Series by L.B. Tillit

Ozzie-Book 1

Zonta-Book 2

Blake-Book 3

Emma-Book 4

Mateo-Book 5

Lilly-Book 6

Lilly

L.B. Tillit

ISBN: 978-1-7352642-6-4
Published in the United States of America

Dedication

To all who face survival on their own and to others who dare to give them lifelines.

Chapter 1

Alone

"No way!" I shoved the outside of the locker room window one more time. It didn't move. It had always moved before. It had always opened for me on days that I needed it to. It was my hideout. My safe space. Had someone checked the locks on the windows of the small locker room? Had someone fixed the broken lock?

I knew it would happen sooner or later. But the timing was really bad!

The rain began to pour as I leaned my head against the frosted window. My socks and shoes were soggy, and my leggings weren't much better. I was afraid my camo backpack was going to be soaked through. I had to find a dry place soon, or all the stuff inside it would be wet too.

I had to think.

I ran to the only place close enough where I could get out of the rain—Hancock High's football stadium. The concrete bleachers rose up against the dark grey sky. I hurried under the bleachers and threw my wet backpack onto a dry concrete slab in front of a snack bar. Of course, the wooden snack bar was boarded up. There weren't any tables or benches under the bleachers since the school didn't want to make it easy for students to hang out. I plopped down next to my bag and sat under the snack bar's sign that read "CLOSED." I was dripping wet, so I opened my backpack and pulled out my blue sweater. It was a little wet, but not as wet as the Food Time Grocery T-shirt I was wearing. I yanked my work T-shirt off and quickly pulled on the sweater.

I didn't bother to see if anyone was watching. Because I knew the answer.

It was the first Monday of Hancock High's Spring Break.

And I was alone.

Chapter 2

Safe

I didn't know what to do or where to go—at least at that very moment. But that was nothing new to me. I was used to having one focus in my life—how do I make it through the next hour? If I was lucky, I could worry about a day at a time. But at that moment, I wasn't lucky.

Staying safe was never easy.

On any day, really.

But Spring Break was one of the worst. For most, Spring Break was a time to relax or go away to a beach somewhere. For most, it meant time with family or friends. For most, it was fun.

Not for me. For me, it meant I had one less place I could feel safe during the day. Hancock High. It was the one safe space I could count on. But at that moment, the school building was closed during Spring Break. This meant no free breakfast or lunch. AND, at that moment, I realized it meant I couldn't sneak into the small locker room to sleep on the nights that I needed to.

At the beginning of the semester, I asked some girls in P.E. about a door that was tucked away in the corner of the gym. They told me it was used for visiting teams when Hancock High had home basketball games or wrestling meets. So, one day, after class, I snuck into the visitor locker room and waited. I waited until school was out and tried to figure out how I could get back in when I needed to. I was excited to find one of the frosted windows had a broken lock. It opened easily for me from the outside. Until I needed it more than ever.

I heard a loud *quack*. I sighed as I opened my backpack again. There was a second loud *quack*. I reached in and grabbed my phone—thankful it was still dry. I still couldn't believe I had listened to my friends Ozzie and Zonta. They told me that I could use my own money to get a phone and only buy the minutes I wanted to buy. That way, I could always reach them if I needed them. It was a way for them to stop worrying about me—a way for them to know that I was safe.

The fact was that Zonta's family had taken me in last Christmas and had tried to give me a phone, but I didn't take it. I didn't want charity, and I didn't want them having eyes on me every minute. They weren't my family. A part of me felt bad, and I guess that was why I agreed to buy my own phone.

I looked down at the text and smiled.

first day of spring break and i don't ever want to ride a horse again

It was from Ozzie. He'd sent a picture, too, of himself on a horse with his mouth wide open like he was screaming. The cowboy hat he was wearing made his large head look even bigger.

LOL. thought you said being a cowboy was in ur DNA

Ozzie's family had driven a few hours west to the Delgado Dude Ranch to attempt a "real" family vacation. Ozzie had told me all about the black cowboys that had tamed the Delgado Mountains. The trip was a way to heal after Ozzie had scared his family last winter by deciding not to live anymore. Thinking about that day still made my stomach turn. He was an all-star football player that seemed to have it together. He was even a big, good-looking guy, although I would never tell him that. But even with his so-called great life, he'd gone through some really dark times. I was glad he'd come out strong on the other side.

Sometimes I wondered what I would have done if Ozzie had gone through with it. I pushed away the thought. He was still here and he was still my friend. Even more of a friend than I could ever have imagined.

i didn't get the riding gene, but i do love these big-ole-hats

I snorted.

LOL. not sure you need 2 have a bigger head than u already do!!!

LOL

What abt ur browns cap? i think it will get jealous

Ozzie never wore anything on his head but the old Cleveland Browns cap his father gave him when he was a kid. Ozzie sent a pic of his Browns cap looped through his belt.

LOL i think my cap is ok w a break

I sat there staring at Ozzie's face with that stupid cowboy hat on. He was happy. I was happy that he was happy. I looked out at the pouring rain, and that moment of joy was gone. Suddenly, I heard a *quack* again. I should never have allowed Zonta to pick my text's ringtone. But it was funny. Not much else was funny, so I left the ringtone alone.

u good?

There it was. He couldn't help but ask me how I was doing. It was what made Ozzie different than others. He wasn't focused only on himself. At least, not anymore. He seemed different when I first met him, but then he'd been a jerk. I just didn't know back then that he was in a dark place. It didn't take me long to forgive him and move on.

yeah, good enough

It was the best answer I could give. I didn't want him to worry, but I didn't want to lie. Not to Ozzie. I didn't want him to be upset with me. I wasn't sure why it mattered so much since he had his life, and it wasn't even close to mine. Still, he was kind and real with me.

good enough? does that mean bad?

I smiled—he knew me too well.

the rain really sucks

Not a lie.

yeah. heard it was raining. BUT it's pretty up here

Suddenly I saw a pic of blue skies and a mountain range.

showoff

can't help it

LOL

u going to be ok?

u know me! got a plan

I should have said *HAD* a plan. But the text was close enough. In fact, I thought I had a good plan to get through Spring Break. I had been excited to get extra hours that week at Food Time Grocery. Stew, my boss, expected me every day that week. From 9 to 2. I usually only worked weekends there and then at Hancock Burger during the week, from 8 p.m. to close, which was around 10 p.m. So, my plan was to mostly live in the little locker room and then make sure I made it to work. Not a problem, right? Wrong!

a plan is good

yes, a plan IS good

I just needed a new plan.

hey ttyl ok?

k

I suddenly felt very alone. That was the problem with having the phone. Before I had it, I didn't know what it meant to have friends checking on me or people who cared enough to even send stupid cowboy hat pics. But when we were done texting, I was always thrown back into my real world.

I turned the power off and shoved the phone back into the middle of my backpack. I told myself that I didn't know where I would be able to charge it next. But reality was I didn't know if I could handle any more texts from Ozzie—not until I had a new plan.

Chapter 3
Just Rain

As I watched the rain pour down, I wrung out my wet T-shirt and hung it over a railing that looped along the walkway near the snack bar. I didn't know how I'd pull it off, but it had to be dry before the next day. I needed it for work at Food Time Grocery.

I grabbed my backpack and paused. The blue ribbon I had tied onto one of the straps was soaked and the color had faded some. My granny had given it to me before she died. I smiled. It had weathered a lot of storms. Today would be no different.

I opened my backpack again and began pulling out the rest of my stuff, thankful it was all still dry. I tested out the power on my flashlight and ran a small brush through my wet hair. I pulled out one of three granola bars and shoved the other two back into the bottom of the bag where I had one change of underwear, a bra, a toothbrush and a small tube of toothpaste, my phone charger, a pair of fuzzy green pj bottoms, and an extra pack of batteries for the flashlight.

I quickly peeled off my wet leggings, slipped on the dry pj bottoms, and hung the leggings next to my wet T-shirt. Before I shoved my stuff back into the pack, I pulled out a small watch from my inside pocket.

It was 3 p.m. I had five hours before I had to be at Hancock Burger.

If the rain stopped, I could maybe figure out a way to dry off. But if it didn't? Would my boss, June, let me come to work with my hair soaked? How could it possibly matter when all I did was bus the tables at Hancock Burger. But what about my soaked leggings and shoes? I had stashed most of my extra clothes in a couple of the lockers in the locker room. The one I couldn't get into anymore. I was sure I couldn't get away with wearing my dry fuzzy green pj bottoms to work.

I took a deep breath and calmed myself down. I told myself I had been through worse. This was nothing. Just rain. So, I set the alarm on my watch to go off in three hours. I could have used the alarm on my phone, but I never did unless I had power. My cheap little watch was more reliable. I chomped down my granola bar before I leaned my head back against the snack bar to try to go to sleep.

I had no idea what I was going to do after work that night, so I had to get sleep when I could—I'd find a safe place later. I couldn't worry anymore at that moment. I needed sleep.

As I drifted off, I told myself, *this is nothing new*.

Chapter 4

Late

"You're late!" June fussed at me as I came in the back door.

"Sorry, June," I answered. "I was hoping the rain would stop. But it didn't." I dropped my backpack onto the floor of the large walk-in supply closet and grabbed a handful of paper towels off the shelf. The space also doubled as a makeshift locker room for the employees.

My boss crossed her arms and stared at me. "What're you doing?"

I didn't even look at her as I pressed the towels against my hair. "Drying off."

"Have you ever heard of an umbrella?" June asked. I looked up and saw the skinny, old, white lady cross her arms. Her almost all-white short hair was slicked back and made her look tough. But her hair net reminded me that she flipped burgers all day. It reminded me that she needed me—at least, I hoped so.

I forced a laugh as I grabbed more towels and pressed them against my leggings. It had been a real challenge to pull them on again after my nap since they were still damp. But as much as I wanted to wear my green pj bottoms, there was no way June would have approved of them. Besides, I could more easily argue my way through wet leggings. "Yeah, but I left my umbrella at home." It wasn't really a lie. The one umbrella my Aunt Clara and I shared was still at home. Although I was pretty sure it had a huge hole. And then there was the fact that I hadn't been home in over a week.

"Well, *think* next time," June snapped. "And hurry up with . . . with whatever you're doing. I've got tables that need to be bussed." Without waiting for me to respond, she turned and left me alone in the large supply closet.

I took a deep breath, thankful she wasn't staring at me anymore. I promised myself that I would never be ashamed—never let anyone make me feel less than. But I had come pretty close to letting shame slip in as I dried off with paper towels in front of my boss. But I had pulled it off and pretended it was no big deal. It had worked.

"Lilly, what're you doing?" Someone else had walked into the supply closet. I was bent over as I pressed one more handful of towels against my leggings. I looked up. In a flash, my cheeks grew warm. Just when I thought I had pulled it off, I was suddenly embarrassed.

It was Mateo Meza-Moya, the quiet Hispanic boy who mostly kept to himself. It was Mateo, the boy who found me hiding in the locker room the week before. It was Mateo who already knew more about me than I wanted him to. "Lilly?" Mateo walked closer to me. "What's going on?"

"Nothing!" I quickly stood up and threw the wet towels in the large trash can in the corner.

"Doesn't look like nothing," Mateo challenged.

"Well, it's none of your business, really." I picked up my backpack, walked over to the far end of the walk-in supply closet, and shoved it in the corner. I didn't want to look into Mateo's dark eyes. He had a way of getting straight to the point. I was okay with straight talk, but only if I was doing it.

"That's right," Mateo shot back. "It's not like I'm covering for you while you decide it's okay to come late and THEN spend another fifteen minutes drying off." I turned around and looked at the big guy. His long dark hair was pulled back in a low ponytail. He held two white earbuds in one hand and a dish rag in the other. "It's not like my band rehearsal really matters." I felt my cheeks warm again. Mateo was part of the Bent Rays, a rock band that had competed a few days earlier. I hadn't even asked him how they did—maybe it wasn't too late.

"How was the Battle of the Bands?" I tried to look interested, but I quickly pulled the wet Food Time Grocery shirt out of my bag and placed it at the top of a mop handle. I hoped June would just think it was a wet rag and leave it alone. I did the mopping anyway, so I wasn't too worried. Maybe it would dry some. Then I grabbed my phone and its charger out of my backpack and plugged it into the wall. I hid the phone behind my bag, even if the plug stuck out of the wall.

I turned and faced Mateo and quickly smiled as soon as I remembered that we were in the middle of a conversation. Since he hadn't answered me the first time, I asked again, "*SO,* how was the Battle of the Bands?"

Mateo just shook his head as he looked me up and down. I wasn't sure if it was a look of disgust or disappointment. I was the one who gave people a good stare-down if they needed one. I never expected to get one from Mateo. "You do *you*, Lilly. That's all that matters." He tossed the dishrag at me. As I caught it, he added, "Table seven needs bussing. Good luck!"

Chapter 5

Table 7

I didn't pay attention to the people that were already heading to Table 7. In fact, I never paid attention to the customers. I focused on grabbing the dirty plates and wiping down the surface before anyone reached the table. I didn't have time to look at, think about, or care about who was going to sit at the table. I was okay with cleaning and moving on. It was almost like a game. Could I get it done before they reached the table? At that moment, I smiled to myself because I lifted the full bussing tub off the table as soon as the customers walked up to my now-clean table. Another win for me.

"Lilly?" I froze, holding the heavy tub as I turned to stare at my Aunt Clara standing next to Table 7. Her too-brown-tanning-bed skin always amazed me. Why couldn't she buy any food for the house, but she could pay for tanning sessions? Over and over again?

"Hi, Aunt Clara," I said as I took a deep breath. At that moment, I saw Kent walk up behind her and put his pale hand around her waist. Kent

Blandon was my Aunt Clara's on-again, off-again boyfriend. Kent liked to party hard with my aunt and use her in whatever way he felt like. If she had any money, he'd hang around and let her pay for everything until it was all gone. If he was suddenly "in love" with her, he'd move in and then break her heart a few months later when he got tired of her and took off.

Most importantly, it was Kent who beat the crap out of me last fall. He was the biggest reason I avoided Aunt Clara's house as much as possible. Over a week ago, he'd moved back in, so I'd been staying in my locker room hideout since then. Until that morning—before I found the locker room window locked.

"Hi, Lilly." Kent gave me his best sales smile. "Where have you been?" Kent was loved by his customers, who bought shoes from him at Hancock Shoes in the Delgado Mall. The customers had no idea what a jerk he was. They saw him as this handsome, fit, white man with long, wavy brown hair. But he was ugly to me. And he always smelled like he took a bath in aftershave. "Are you going to answer me?" Kent reminded me he had asked a question.

I didn't look him in the eyes, and I didn't answer him. In fact, I never spoke to him. Instead, I looked at my aunt and said, "Your table is clean."

I turned to leave, but she reached out her skinny arm to touch my shoulder. "Wait, Lilly." I looked at her hand and frowned. She never touched me. Ever. She quickly removed her hand like I had somehow burned her. "I didn't know you worked here."

I just stared at her. How could I make this fast so I could get away from Table 7? She'd been high when I had her sign the work permit, but she hadn't remembered—and I hadn't reminded her. The less she knew, the better life was for me.

She did remember that I worked at Food Time Grocery, which helped me buy food that I sometimes brought back to the house. On those days that I lived there. It was important that she knew about one of my jobs because I did *not* want her to think I stole money or was part of some illegal scheme. Still, she didn't need to know more than I wanted her to. I simply did not trust her. Then there was the fact that she clearly did NOT care about me, so I really didn't care about her. I took a deep breath and yawned, "Yes, I work here. You signed the papers. Not my problem that you forgot. Got other tables to bus."

"But you said you were going to the beach with the Jones family." Aunt Clara used a sweet voice. Too sweet. I had told her that Zonta and her family had invited me to the beach. But that was all. I still appreciated Zonta and her parents, Monta and Zeb, for taking me in late last winter when Kent beat me up. The Joneses were a great family, but I didn't need any more charity from them. Still, they kept reaching out to me, but going on vacation with them would have been weird.

I never really understood Monta and Zeb's need to show me how much they cared for me since I'd done nothing to deserve it. But Zonta was a different case. We had become close ever since she came to my house and had a glimpse into my world. She didn't push me away like most people did. Up to that point, I thought she had been selfish, but I learned she really didn't know better. After that, our friendship grew—still, I was not ready to go on a Jones family vacation.

"I said I *might* go with them," I answered. "But I didn't go. Did I?"

"Don't talk to your aunt that way!" As expected, Kent's hostile side showed up. But I didn't even look at him. I didn't want to see that spark of anger in his eyes. So, I just kept looking at Aunt Clara as if Kent hadn't said a word.

"Whatever, Lilly." Aunt Clara was done pretending to care. She plopped into a chair. "Just tell the waiter we're ready to order." She looked at Kent and said, "Order what you want. I'm paying for all of us."

Kent sat next to her, leaned over, and kissed her. "Thanks, Babe."

"I'm starving after the weekend we've had." Aunt Clara gave me that look—that look that always meant *I partied hard*. But I just kept my face blank. I was sick of her poor choices, ones that left me without a safe place to sleep.

When I didn't respond, they both looked at the menu, which was tucked under the glass tabletop. It was June's simple idea to save money, but the menu tabletops became a fun part of Hancock Burger.

As the two of them were busy pointing out which burgers they were going to order, I shook my head and finally carried the bussing tub into the kitchen.

Chapter 6

June Figby

A long two-way shelf was built into a slit in the wall between the kitchen and the dining area. Plates filled with burgers and fries were already lined up along the shelf, waiting for the only two waiters to deliver them to the right tables. I peeked through the slit and watched my aunt wave toward the front door. My mouth dropped as I watched her good-for-nothing son, Rick Orem, walk in. His good-for-nothing pregnant girlfriend, Steph Pritt, was behind him with her two-year-old girl, Nova, in tow.

"What's wrong?" June's voice caused me to snap my mouth shut.

"Nothing," I quickly answered as I emptied the tub. There was so much wrong! Not to mention the simple fact that it was almost 8:30. What were all of them doing eating dinner so late with a two-year-old in tow?

"Liar," my boss stated, but she was not fussing at me. She put her hands on her hips and looked through the slit in the wall. "Hmmmm. Let's see who you were looking at."

"Nobody," I lied again as I shoved the handle above the large sink to fill my tub with clean water.

June looked at me and shook her head. "I think that family sitting at Table 7 really bothers you." She snorted at me when I didn't answer and began to search for clean rags. "Calm down, child." She pointed her bony finger into my face. "I don't like everyone that walks in here, either."

There was something about that bony finger pointing at me that got me every time. Got me in a good way—calmed me down. It reminded me of my granny, who used to get my attention that way. I missed her like crazy.

"I know, June," I finally answered. "It's just they *really* bother me. Bad."

June nodded. "How bad?"

Lying wasn't working, so I told her the truth. "They're family."

June laughed out loud. "Well, that's usually the case." She took off her apron and handed it to me. "I think you can flip burgers awhile, and I'll bus. Then, when they're gone, we'll switch back."

"Are we allowed to do that?" I asked.

June laughed again. "I'm the boss, remember?" She reached for my bussing tub.

I couldn't believe my cranky boss was going to switch with me while my family sat on the other side of the wall. "Okay . . . thank you." I tied the apron around my waist and grabbed a hairnet.

"But before I do, you have to tell me one thing." June had a sparkle in her eye—which was weird since she seemed to care less about our personal lives. June Figby was a strange one. But it put me at ease.

"Sure. What?" I asked as I tucked my blond hair into the hairnet.

"What's wrong with them?" She raised her eyebrows like a kid waiting for candy.

I swallowed and glanced through the slit again. Table 7 seemed to be placing a large order since Roy, Hancock Burger's favorite waiter, kept jotting down more and more items. I shook my head. "It's hard to explain."

June whispered, "Try."

I looked at the old lady facing me. I was just a little taller than she was, but barely. I had never noticed the fleck of green in one of her brown eyes. My granny had green eyes like mine—so that speck of green in June's eyes felt like Granny was telling me to trust this lady.

"I have never seen my aunt and her boyfriend eat with her son and his girlfriend," I stated.

June frowned. She was clearly disappointed my story was not more dramatic. "So?"

I reached my hands under the warm running water. Washing them would feel good, but June was still waiting for me to make the trade more interesting. "Okay. My cousin, Rick, thinks his mother—my Aunt Clara—is a sorry drunk. Which she is." I turned off the water and grabbed a paper towel.

June suddenly glanced through the slit—then jerked her head back around and stared at me. I couldn't quite read her. She cleared her throat and said, "And . . . so . . . I see a lot of drunks come and go."

I quickly explained, "The thing is, my aunt doesn't feed anyone. Not herself, not her son or his kids, and for sure, NOT his girlfriend. And especially *never* me."

"Oh." June frowned. I could suddenly read her loud and clear—she felt pity. It was why I never shared my story.

I quickly added, "So, why is she suddenly paying for a huge meal for everyone? Why would my aunt feed someone else's kid? Nova isn't even Rick's. AND I know as a fact that my aunt's good-for-nothing boyfriend won't be paying a dime."

"Maybe she won the lottery?" June halfway laughed.

"Yeah, right," I grunted. "But knowing her, even if she has won the lottery, she will still ask me to give her a break on the bill since I work here."

"Well, we can't have that." June smiled and winked at me. "I'll keep an eye on them."

I watched June walk out of the kitchen door, ready to bus my tables. As I turned to flip burgers, I suddenly felt uneasy. Where did Aunt Clara get the money? Had she crossed over from partying to dealing? Was there a chance I could never sleep at her house again? But there was one thing I did know. As long as Kent Blandon lived with Aunt Clara, I wouldn't have a place to sleep.

Chapter 7
Options

I was thankful that Mateo had already left. It was good he didn't hear me spill the details about my world to June. Only a few hours earlier, he had said, *"You do you, Lilly. That's all that matters."* He clearly believed that I only thought of myself. Which was true—and I hated that. But how could I worry about someone else's feelings or schedules or anything? The fact was, I couldn't. I was making everything up from hour to hour. I had to think of me first. I had to survive. Was that so wrong?

I pushed Mateo's judging words out of my mind, and I stepped out of Hancock Burger at 10 p.m. My still-wet Food Time Grocery T-shirt was wrapped in paper towels. I had shoved it into a plastic bag and tied it to the bottom of my backpack. I knew it would really smell bad in the morning, but I didn't let myself go there. I had to focus on now—not tomorrow. My phone was also tightly wrapped inside a plastic bag that I'd grabbed from the storage closet. But it was tucked into my dry pj bottoms in the backpack. It was fully charged, so I could use it if I needed to. The last thing I carried was another plastic bag with two burgers and a pile of leftover fries. I always took leftovers. Always.

June and Roy were inside, locking up. I liked to stand at the door for a minute so I could hear the two of them laugh. When it was a slow night, Roy would talk to June through the slit in the wall between the dining room and kitchen. She would snap out of her grumpy mood and laugh. I missed the ease of laughter—especially with my granny.

As I stepped away from Hancock Burger, I pretended that I knew where I was going as I headed toward the bus stop. No one was watching me, but I still pretended. It made me feel better to think that I knew where I was going.

As I got closer to the road, I decided I would head back to the stadium. I had never slept under the bleachers before. At least, not at night. I had thought about taking Bus 51 West two blocks to Oak Park. There was a large wooden pirate ship in the center of the playground that always welcomed me.

In the middle of the ship, there was an opening with steps that led into the belly of the ship. I would sleep along the low-to-the-ground wooden benches that didn't smell too bad. I loved that a chain-link fence wrapped around the park, and it had a large sign that read *Closed from Dusk to Dawn*. It kept people away and made me feel safe. At least, I believed that I was safe. But after heavy rains, it would be wet inside the belly of the ship. After all, it was just a playground. So, that night, Oak Park was *not* an option.

The rain started again as I walked quickly back to the stadium, eager to get the night over with. The stadium seemed so dark as I got closer to it. Streetlights lit up enough of the tall structure to see where I was going. But I couldn't see all the way to the spot where I had taken a nap that afternoon. Without daylight or the huge stadium lights, the place suddenly creeped me out.

As soon as I reached the familiar spot, I reached into my backpack and pulled out my flashlight. It was more like a lantern and didn't have the strongest beam. Still, it lit up enough of the dry space for my heart to begin to race. I was not alone.

Chapter 8

Others

"What do you want?" A white woman who might have been in her twenties stumbled toward me. Two men sat on the ground and were leaning up against the closed snack bar, just like I had done that afternoon. A couple of sleeping bags and two other large bags were lying next to them. One man was a pretty big Hispanic guy, probably the woman's age. He had his arms crossed as he stared at me. The other one was an older white guy with a rough-looking black beard who was more interested in whatever was in the brown bag he was holding.

"Nothing," I answered as I began to back up. Slowly.

"I don't believe you!" The woman got closer as I kept stepping back. Two more steps, and I'd be standing in the rain again. I had run into homeless people over the years, but I had quickly learned what areas to avoid when I needed a place to sleep. Homeless people sleeping under the stadium was new to me. I'd learned that some people hung out under bridges that crossed the Rayo River. Sometimes, spots had just one loner, and other places could have a dozen. Then there were a few abandoned buildings, like the old video store, where some people slept or hung out until they were chased off. But those areas were close to the center of Hancock. As was the one shelter where some homeless headed when they really wanted a bed.

Ruth's Place was a well-known shelter in Hancock. It was located on the corner of Winters Street and 3rd Avenue. I had been given that address more times than I can remember, but I told myself I didn't need it. I had a home. I just wanted to pick and choose when I'd sleep there.

I wondered why these guys were this far north. Didn't they know it was school property? Didn't they know they were trespassing? I was sure someone would call the police on them. Then I caught myself—they were probably just caught in the rain like I was.

"Sorry, I was just walking by," I said as I tried to figure out if it was best to run or just walk away like they didn't exist. But I couldn't do that—I had just spoken to them.

"Ha! That's funny." The old man laughed. He stood up and started walking my way. "It's raining and it's dark." He lifted a dirty finger while his other hand clutched the brown bag. Pointing that dirty finger at me, he added, "You're a liar!"

I took a deep breath. Think, I had to think. I looked straight at the old man and woman and realized they hadn't moved any closer. They were just as confused about me as I was about them. "Yes." I nodded. "I lied."

"I knew it!" The man smiled, happy that he was right. Then he reached into his bag and pulled out a bottle, unscrewed the top, took a swig, and put the bottle back in the bag.

"Well, go on." The woman tried to stand without leaning, but she struggled.

"I thought you might need some food," I lied again, but I hoped they would believe me as I held out my plastic bag with the leftover burgers and fries. "Here."

The woman stared at me for a minute before she reached for my bag. "I'd be careful, Meg," the old man warned.

"Shut up, Nelson!" The woman yelled like she would hit him if he said another word. "I'm hungry! YOU don't have to eat it." Then she looked in the bag. "Oh, smells good." I felt myself begin to relax.

"I don't know." Nelson started again.

Before Meg could scream at Nelson again, the large Hispanic man came up behind her. "I think it's safe," he said calmly as he moved in closer to me.

"What makes you so sure, Rafi?" Nelson came up next to Rafi and stared at me.

By this time, Meg was already eating one of the burgers, happy with the food.

"It's that girl, you know?" He pointed at my backpack. "She's one of us."

"Oh, yeah, the green-camo-backpack-girl," Nelson added.

"What are you talking about?" I asked, the fear beginning to build again.

"You sleep in that playground sometimes. We've seen you." Rafi smiled, but his eyes still scared me. They were intense. He wasn't high or drunk, not from what I could tell, but I almost wished he had been passed out instead of staring at me.

"You've seen me?" I took a step back and felt rain begin to hit my head.

"Yeah, all the time." He nodded but then looked at Meg and grabbed the bag. "Hey, leave some for me!"

That was my chance. I took off running. My backpack felt heavier with each step, and the plastic bag that I had tied on swung so hard that it kept hitting my leg.

I didn't let myself stop running until I heard laughter. They were laughing at me—I was okay with that. But it was very clear that the stadium was no longer an option.

Chapter 9

Bus 51

The rain began to pour again as I headed back toward Hancock Burger. Maybe June and Roy would still be there. But as I got closer, I saw all the lights were out, and their cars were gone. I settled for the small shelter at the bus stop. I stood under the plastic roof that did nothing to keep the rain from blowing in from the sides—I had no idea where to go. There was no way I was heading to Ruth's Place. I was not one of them, no matter what Rafi had said.

Within minutes, Bus 51 Eastbound pulled up. Without thinking, I jumped on. I'd figure out the best option. I just needed time to think. "Wet night!" the bus driver said as I climbed onto Bus 51 and scanned my Hancock-Metro card. He was an older Hispanic guy who looked familiar. His name tag read *Pedro*.

"Yes, sir," I answered as I forced a smile and headed to the back of the bus—my stomach growled. I pulled out a granola bar and ate it, wishing I had at least kept some fries.

There were only a handful of people on the bus and only four more eastbound stops before Bus 51 turned around at Lake Midway and headed west again.

What were my options? If I could, I would have stayed on the bus all night. But that wasn't allowed. I could wait, turn around with the bus, and head back toward Oak Park to stay at the rain-soaked playground. But my Food Time Grocery shirt was still wet, and that was a big problem. If I couldn't hang it up in a dry place, I'd have to wear it wet to work in the morning. And it would stink, too.

At each bus stop, someone got off. There was one more stop, and I felt my heart race. What would I do? I couldn't stay at Lake Midway since there was no shelter there. It was the rich neighborhood, and none of the families would be happy to see me tucked into one of their boat houses along the shore.

"Miss?" Pedro yelled to the back of the bus. We had arrived at the final stop. "Last stop," he yelled like he did every day.

I nodded, stood up, and walked toward the door. The rain was coming down hard. I stopped at the top of the steps and sighed. "I think I need to head the other direction. I made a mistake and went the wrong way. I need to get off at the Oak Park stop." I decided that uncomfortable-wet in a safe place was better than walking around out in the open rain. I'd just deal with a stinky wet shirt in the morning. It wouldn't be the first time I had stunk in public. But then I remembered what Rafi had said. They had been watching me. Who else was watching me? The fact was that Oak Park was never going to be my safe place again. I felt a chill hit me when I realized it never had been.

Pedro frowned. "Are you okay, Miss?"

I forced the smile again. "Yes, I'm . . . I'm just upset because I went the wrong way. I'm sorry." I felt my cheeks warm. I had outright lied. It wasn't even a half-truth or a short little throw-away lie, like when I told June nothing was wrong. This was a full-on lie.

Pedro did not smile. He knew, but he was the bus driver, not my parent. "Okay." I began to pull out my Hancock-Metro Card again, but he waved his hand. "No, it's okay." He pointed at the seat behind him. "Just sit down and let's get you home."

Home.

It felt like a slap.

Home.

Something began to break.

Home.

I quickly sat down and took a breath. That word would NOT break me. But even if I had wanted to say something to Pedro, I couldn't. If I opened my mouth, I would break down and cry. But I could not do that. I had to survive.

One hour at a time.

I leaned my head against the window and watched the rain hit the glass hard, making it look like small rivers trying to break into the dry safety of the bus. The dry safety zone I'd soon have to leave.

As we pulled up to the second stop on the way back toward the West side of town, I noticed a bus pull in behind us.

I took a deep breath, finally daring to speak. "What bus is that?" I asked Pedro.

"Southbound Bus 66," he answered as he began to pull into the stop to pick up an older man and his dog. "It stops at the same bus stop."

Bus 66.

I knew that bus! And I knew where Bus 66 could take me. "I'm getting off here!" I stated before he closed the door behind the dog that was shaking out his fur. Water splashed all over my clothes—which didn't matter since they were already nasty wet.

"But this is not Oak Park," he argued.

I smiled. "Yes, I know, but I was wrong. I need to head south." I jumped off before Pedro could say anything else, and I didn't look back because I didn't want to see the look on his face. I didn't want to see his reaction to the second lie that I had fed him.

I jumped onto Bus 66 and smiled as it headed south. For the first time that night, I knew exactly where I was going. There was one person that might not care if I showed up wet and nasty and in need—in the middle of the night.

Vashon Wilkes.

Yes, I'd go to Vashon Wilkes's home. He was always there for me. Why would this night be any different?

Chapter 10

Vashon

As soon as I sat down, I dug into my backpack and pulled out my phone.

vashon u still up?

I stared at my text for a whole minute as Bus 66 headed south.

Vashon Wilkes was a freshman at Hancock High. When I showed up that first week at school last fall, he spoke to me right away at lunch. As a junior, it was my first year at Hancock High. I didn't know anyone, but I was okay with that. I'd gone to Hemby High off and on. It was the biggest sport's rival to Hancock High. But I didn't care much about sports. I felt it was a luxury. Something that people did if they had their life together.

When I was 14, Granny died, and I learned very quickly that I should care about one thing and one thing only. Did I have what I needed so I could make it on my own when I turned 18?

Granny and teachers had told me early on that school was important. If I couldn't read or write or do math, then it would be harder to survive. I didn't understand what they meant at first. But once I moved in with Aunt Clara, I quickly learned.

Aunt Clara didn't make it easy for me to get to school every day when we lived in Hemby. She worked late and needed to sleep in. She didn't care if I did or didn't go to school. She didn't even care if I ate enough food or not. So, my grades dropped and I was hungry a whole lot.

It was weird, though, because I started gaining weight. I ate what I could when I could, and it didn't matter what it was. I didn't care, though, if I was chubby. I felt like a little extra weight made it look to others like I wasn't hungry all the time. It made them think I just had too much to eat. And I wanted them to keep thinking that because I didn't want to be pitied.

When I saw that Aunt Clara didn't care, I had to take matters into my own hands and find a way to get to school. At age 14, I found out which school bus stopped near my house. At age 14, I talked to teachers who worked with me to make up missed work. At age 14, I learned how to take extra food home from the lunchroom so I could eat at night. At age 14, I learned that I had to take control of my life because Aunt Clara sure didn't care.

But Vashon cared right away. The minute he met me, he shared his lunch and made me smile. He made everyone smile. So, I sat with him at lunch and told him more things about my life than anyone else. If there was anyone that I trusted, it was Vashon.

I decided to text him again. Maybe he just didn't hear the first text come through.

HELLO VASHON!!!!!! r you home? r u up?

Was he not home? Had Vashon's family gone on vacation like everyone else? I didn't think so, since his granny was raising him *and* his three younger brothers.

Maybe his phone was just off. That was what I told myself as I got off at the bus stop on Hall Drive. I knew the Hall community because I'd been to Vashon's a couple of times. I only had to walk one block before I'd turn left onto his road. He lived in a house right at the beginning of Hall Circle. Ozzie just lived on the other side of the Hall Circle loop. But walking through any neighborhood in the middle of the night, in the rain, was just not my smartest move. But I didn't know where else to go or what to do.

I hesitated as I stood at the Wilkes's front door. I was soaking wet and beginning to get chilled. I saw Mrs. Wilkes's car sitting in the driveway—they were home. That was a good sign. At least, I hoped so. The house was dark, and I suddenly wondered if I was making a mistake. If I knocked on the door, I'd wake up everyone who was sleeping. Vashon's granny would be pissed. From what Vashon had told me, it was never good to make Mrs. Wilkes angry.

But I was tired, wet, and out of options.

Suddenly, I heard Vashon laugh. I looked to my left and saw one of the windows flash blue lights. I felt my whole body relax. Vashon was awake and probably gaming, so I didn't have to wake up the whole house. I just had to get Vashon to let me in.

I walked in the pouring rain toward his window. I didn't care anymore about everything getting soaked in my backpack since it was most likely all wet at that point.

But I felt hope as I reached the window that had a blue light flickering. So, I knocked.

Chapter 11

Ask

At first, there was silence. Then the room went dark. No more blue lights and no more laughter. So, I knocked on Vashon's window again and whispered as loudly as I could, "Vashon? Hey, Vashon!"

Two fingers poked between two blinds and slowly parted the metal. Two eyes suddenly stared through the slit in the blinds. Within seconds, the blinds pulled up, and the window opened. "Lilly? What's wrong? Are you hurt?"

"No. I'm fine, but I'm soaked. I need a place to crash for the night. Got to dry off for work tomorrow." It felt good telling the truth.

Vashon's lanky arm reached through the window, and he grabbed my backpack. "Are you crazy? It's 11:30! Get in here, girl." He dropped the backpack somewhere in the dark and then reached back out and grabbed my two arms to try to pull me in. But he wasn't strong enough, so I grabbed a tree branch that hung near his window and awkwardly climbed into his room.

"Thanks, Vashon," I said as he closed the window behind me. "Tried to text you first." I raised my voice. "Seems you were too busy to—"

"Shhhhh, don't wake up Granny," He whispered and reached for something in the dark. Suddenly, a small lamp filled the room with an orange glow. Vashon's room wasn't very big, but he was happy not to share it with any of his three younger brothers. Vashon plopped down into his rolling chair. It leaned up against a long folding table set up along the wall opposite his bed. "I was gaming." He smiled as he pointed at the two computer monitors and gaming gear that took up most of the space.

"I thought so," I whispered and then shivered.

Vashon's smile vanished. "What's wrong with you?" He suddenly remembered he had pulled me through his window. "I thought you were done running away in the middle of the night."

My cheeks warmed. "I'm not running away." Then I whispered, trying to remind him, "I tried to text you first. Remember?"

Vashon stood up and crossed his arms as he looked down at me. He had never looked down on me before. I realized the skinny black kid I had met last fall was growing. "If you're not running away again, then what do you call running around in the middle of the night in a strange neighborhood?"

"It's not strange," I argued. "I know *you*."

Vashon rolled his eyes. "Point is, you shouldn't be in any neighborhood wandering around."

"I wasn't wandering. I came straight to you." In a roundabout sort of way, but I didn't tell him that.

Vashon looked at his door and back at me as he shook his head. "You can't stay." My mouth dropped open. Vashon started opening the drawers of a small dresser next to the bed. "Let me see if I have some dry clothes you can take with you . . . that might fit you." He grabbed a green striped shirt and held it up to me.

I stared at the small shirt that would never fit. "Are you kidding me?"

Vashon dropped his hand, still holding the shirt. "Look, I can't upset Granny. If she finds you in here with me, she will kill me!" He rolled his eyes. "Worse than kill me. She'd take away my computer setup and not let me help Bent Rays anymore. I can't risk it." He hung his head and added, "I'm so sorry."

I forgot Vashon had been helping Mateo's band with social media marketing. Vashon gently touched the monitor closest to him. I realized that even though Vashon helped me when he could, he had a life. A life he wasn't willing to sacrifice for me.

I turned away from him and faced the window I had just climbed through. I could see the rain was not letting up. I had to think. I had to find a way. I had to survive. Suddenly, I had an idea.

I swung back around. "What if you asked her?"

This time, Vashon's mouth dropped open. "What?"

"Ask your granny if I can stay." I pointed at his door. "Go right now and wake her up and tell her you have a problem. That I came knocking on your window, and you don't know what to do with me."

"But she might get upset." Vashon shook his head.

"But since it's the truth, she won't be upset. You're hiding nothing from her." I kept pushing Vashon. Mrs. Wilkes was a fierce woman you didn't mess with. But she also had a big heart and did what was right.

A smile grew on Vashon's face. "You're right. That might work."

"It worked before when you asked her to help Zonta!" I added. In January, Mrs. Wilkes helped Zonta get away from a party where a jerk was going to hurt her. According to Zonta, Mrs. Wilkes did not hesitate when Vashon asked her to take Zonta home from the party.

"True!" Vashon nodded and didn't wait a second longer to head out his door. Before he closed it behind him, he popped his head back through and whispered, "Don't move! Stay right there!" I rolled my eyes as he shut the door. There was no way I was moving.

As I stood waiting, I could hear the rain hitting the windows behind me. I took two deep breaths as my heart began to beat faster. Would Mrs. Wilkes scream and yell at Vashon? Would she kick me out? But then I remembered one more thing Zonta had told me about Mrs. Wilkes. She had given Zonta's mother, Monta, a talking-to, which caused Monta to finally take Zonta's issues seriously.

I was counting on the same wise woman walking through Vashon's door to help me.

Chapter 12

Mrs. Wilkes

Within minutes, I heard voices growing louder and louder before Vashon's door flew open. "Oh, my Lord!" Mrs. Wilkes clutched her purple bathrobe and patted down the smooth silk scarf that was wrapped around her head. One small, pink curling rod tried to poke through right above her eye. She found it and shoved it back under the scarf. "Lilly! You look like a mess."

"I am a mess," I stated as I stared at the only adult who could help me.

"Well, don't just stand there." She came over to me and put her arm around my shoulder. She was about my height, so her dark eyes looked straight into mine as she guided me through Vashon's room and out into the hall. "Going to get you a nice shower and some dry clothes."

"Okay," was all I managed to say. Vashon just stared at his granny as she huddled over me like a mother hen.

"Vashon!" Mrs. Wilkes raised her voice. "Pick up that backpack and bring it to me in the kitchen."

"Yes, ma'am." Vashon jumped into action. He lifted my backpack like it was nasty and held it out in front of him as he tried to avoid the swinging plastic bag that still held my wet T-shirt. I wasn't quite sure what Mrs. Wilkes planned to do with my backpack but I didn't care. I was going to be clean and dry. At least for one night.

Chapter 13

Sleepover

Some people might say that it would be strange to sleep on someone else's couch. Some might think it strange to wear someone else's oversized old lady pjs that smelled like soap. Others might think it strange to be surrounded by wall decorations and family pics that didn't include them. But to me, it was not strange. It was *not* my first couch or first home where people were kind enough to take me in. In fact, I stopped counting once I realized that counting only made me feel worse. So, I just focused on a moment at a time.

At that moment, I could hear the washing machine hum from the corner of the kitchen. Mrs. Wilkes had me empty my backpack and dump any clothes into the washing machine before she prepared the couch and gave me a clean towel and a pair of her pjs.

Vashon had been shooed off to bed, which he was happy to do. Mrs. Wilkes said that we'd talk in the morning. I was fine with that. There was always the morning. A new day to make a new plan.

But at that moment, I was warm and dry. That's all that mattered as the rhythm of the washing machine lulled me to sleep.

Chapter 14

Bacon & Eggs

My stomach growled as the smell of bacon and eggs woke me. "GRANNY, SHE'S AWAKE!" Vashon's youngest brother was right up in my face, pointing his finger at me. His dark skin wasn't the only thing he had in common with Vashon. He had the same wide smile, except two teeth were missing.

"Legend, stop yelling." Vashon towered over his brother. He smiled at me, "Sorry about that. He's only 6."

As I sat up, I realized Legend wasn't the only one staring at me. Two other boys, one skinny like Vashon and one a little on the chubby side, sat at the end of the couch at my feet. The ten-year-old chubby one smiled and asked, "Are you Vashon's girlfriend?"

Vashon slapped his head. "Shut up, Bear. You know she's my friend. She's been here before."

"Don't hit your brother!" Granny yelled from the kitchen.

"Hi, Lilly, remember me? Caleb." Vashon's twelve-year-old brother held out his hand to me.

I smiled as I shook his hand. "Yes, I do. *Caleb.*"

"He's the only one with manners," Vashon explained.

"That includes you!" Bear stuck his tongue out at Vashon. "I think she *is* your girl since she spent the night this time!"

Vashon raised his hand to hit Bear again when Mrs. Wilkes yelled, "Get yourselves in here for some breakfast." The boys jumped up and headed around the corner into the kitchen as Bear stuck his tongue out at Vashon one more time. "I saw that!" Mrs. Wilkes fussed. "Didn't I raise you better?"

I could hear Bear whisper, "Yes, ma'am."

Mrs. Wilkes raised her voice. "Breakfast is for you too, Lilly. I left you a bathrobe to wear."

With the boys all around the corner in the kitchen, I awkwardly pulled my covers off and noticed a light purple bathrobe across the top of the couch. Although I had been many places, I had never worn a bathrobe before. Ever. But the bacon and eggs smelled good, so I pulled the robe over my borrowed pj's and zipped it up. I looked like one huge purple gumdrop, but I didn't care.

As I came around the corner into the open kitchen, the boys all giggled, including Vashon. I put my hands on my hips. "What? Don't you think I look great?"

Mrs. Wilkes turned toward me holding a plate full of bacon in her hand. Her dark brown hair had striking white streaks that fell in perfect waves down to her chin. She looked like she'd just walked out of the hairdresser. She had a bright yellow apron covering her classic blue business pants and a white blouse. She'd transformed from a granny into a classy businesswoman.

"You look like Granny!" Bear laughed. I couldn't argue since he was right. It looked like Mrs. Wilkes had morphed into a chubby white girl overnight. Except, I didn't have my hair up in rods. In fact, I was pretty sure my hair was a blond tangled mess at that moment.

"What's so wrong with that?" Mrs. Wilkes frowned at the boy as she carried the bacon to the table.

Bear quickly dropped his head as she sat down. "Nothing."

The rest of the boys laughed, and Mrs. Wilkes patted Bear's head. "That's what I thought."

I couldn't help but smile as I watched Mrs. Wilkes command her grandsons. She grinned at me and waved at the table. "Sit, sit!" So, I did. Suddenly, everyone was quiet as Mrs. Wilkes said a quick prayer. As soon as she finished, everyone began to reach for food.

Vashon nodded at me to grab some food, too, which I did.

It was the best breakfast I had eaten since I lived with Zonta's family. As I took a bite of toast with some jelly, Mrs. Wilkes cleared her throat. "Well, Lilly. It's morning, so let's talk about what you're going to do next?"

The toast suddenly stuck in my throat, so I grabbed the glass of juice in front of me to wash it down. "Now? You want to talk in front of all of them?" I pointed at Vashon and all his brothers staring at me.

"Well, you brought your world into theirs. It's only fair." Mrs. Wilkes smiled, and I could tell she wasn't being mean. She was stating a fact. "I never miss a moment to teach my boys about real life."

Real life. Was it real life for them? Would it ever be? I felt my cheeks warm, but I was not going to argue with her. "Okay, well, I hope to go to work at Food Time Grocery." Suddenly, my eyes grew wide. "Oh, no, I forgot. I need to dry my clothes. Do we have time—"

"They're dry." Mrs. Wilkes pointed at a small, folded pile on the washing machine in the corner. My Food Time Grocery shirt was clean and dry on top of the pile. She'd even washed my fuzzy green pjs and all the clothes I had on yesterday, including my blue sweater. I frowned when I saw other things, like my flashlight and watch, sitting neatly next to the clothes. Before I could ask, Mrs. Wilkes added, "Your backpack is in the dryer now."

"Thank you," I whispered. I couldn't believe that she'd washed my backpack too. How long had she been awake? Drying *all* my stuff, getting dressed up, and making breakfast. A lump grew in my throat. For a moment, I remembered what it felt like for someone to care.

"Well, what are you going to do after work?" She pushed, clearly not going to let me get away with being vague.

"I have a second job at night at Hancock Burger." I smiled. "I'm excited that I get to work all Spring Break. I'll make some extra money."

"And then?" Mrs. Wilkes took another bite of bacon and wiped her mouth with a cloth napkin.

"What do you mean?" I reached for the cloth napkin next to my plate and carefully spread it out in my lap. I couldn't remember the last time I had used a cloth napkin.

I knew what she meant, but I needed her to ask it. I needed to know where she stood. So, I wasn't surprised when she asked, "Where will you sleep each night? Are you going home?"

There it was. I didn't want to lie to her, but I also didn't want her to think I'd show up at her house every night. She wanted to know if I had a plan and how much of my plan might include her. She wanted to have a say so I wouldn't rope her into something she wasn't willing to do.

It was always the same. Some people were ready for me to move in, and others were ready for me never to stay over again. I thought maybe Mrs. Wilkes hadn't quite decided which one she would be, but I didn't want her to make that decision.

"I'll head to my cousin's tonight," I quickly answered. I hadn't planned to, but I realized that maybe it was my only choice at that point, at least until Spring Break was over. Staying with my good-for-nothing cousin, Rick, was not ideal, but it would buy me time to talk to Zonta when she got back from her trip to the beach. Maybe her parents, Monta and Zeb, were still willing to let me stay with them for a little while again. But only until I could figure out a better option.

"Okay, good." Mrs. Wilkes smiled and reached her hand out to squeeze my hand. "If you ever need to stay over in an emergency again, you have a place with us."

There it was. She was okay with playing the emergency part. I looked at the four growing boys and knew that she could only offer so much. Another mouth to feed might not allow her to give her boys everything she wanted them to have.

"Thank you." I squeezed her hand back. "That means a lot." I meant it. I would take *emergency* over *never again* any day.

Chapter 15

Blake

"Blake," I called out as he walked by me down the coffee aisle.

"What's up?" Blake stopped and looked down at me as I shoved a bag of coffee beans onto the bottom shelf.

"Are you going home after work today?" I asked as if I was asking him about the weather.

Blake frowned and focused on the coffee, not me. "Yes, I am. Why?" He glanced at me and then away again. I was used to Blake's body language.

At the beginning of the year, people thought he was a jerk. He hung out with the wrong crowd and said a whole lot of awful things to fit in. As a blond-haired, blue-eyed white boy, he said some pretty racist things in History class that didn't sit well with others. In fact, the comments caused him to get beat up.

But something in Blake changed. Even I was surprised that he stood up to his so-called friends. He even protected Zonta from being hurt by Carlos, a guy we all thought was Blake's best friend.

It was soon after that, when Blake was on his own, that he shared that he has autism. He made new friends, placed 5th in the State Wrestling Championship, and had a girlfriend.

It was Blake who helped me get the job at Food Time Grocery. But it was the fact that Blake lived in Hancock's public housing that mattered to me the most at that moment. A few months ago, he'd seen me in the stairwell of his building, arguing with my cousin Rick. At the time, I was still living with Aunt Clara, Rick's mother. But I had been so hungry that I begged my cousin for money. I still hated that Blake heard me that day. I hated that he knew how hungry I had been. But it had been the reason he helped me get the job at Food Time Grocery, so I quickly got over it.

"I need to get into your building so I can get to my cousin's apartment," I stated as I grabbed another bag of coffee.

"Can't you just call him or have him let you in with the intercom?" Blake asked.

"He won't let me in if he knows it's me."

"Then why do you want to go in if he's going to yell at you again?" Blake frowned. He had a point, but I hoped Rick wouldn't yell this time.

"I need a place to stay through the rest of this week," I stated. "I hope that if I can talk to him face to face, he will listen this time."

"Why would he listen this time?" Blake frowned and watched me shove another coffee bag onto the shelf.

"Because I don't need his money this time." But what I didn't tell Blake was that I would also offer him $200 from this week's check if he let me stay the week. It might convince him.

"Okay, I'll let you in," Blake said and began to head down the aisle toward the back of the store. But then he stopped and turned to face me. "I'll see you at the bus stop after work. We'll take the 2:15 bus." If I could get things worked out with my cousin, then I'd still have plenty of time to get to Hancock Burger by 8 p.m.

"I'll be there." I smiled as Blake nodded and walked away. Blake would do exactly what he said he'd do. Knowing I could count on him, even if it was just to let me into his building, made me feel different. Different from yesterday. I shook my head and smiled. Such a simple thing as taking the bus with Blake to his neighborhood made me feel safe. It may have still been a long shot, and Rick Orem was not the best person in the world. But having a plan, and knowing I was heading into the plan with Blake, offered me a moment where I didn't feel so alone.

Chapter 16

What Happened?

"Why is Ms. Williams mad at you?" Blake suddenly asked as we sat next to each other on Bus 51 headed along Hillview Avenue. Hillview apartments were only a few blocks away.

"What?" I was surprised by his question. Ms. Williams was our U.S. History teacher, and I hadn't thought about her since our Spring Break started. I had other things to worry about, and she was not a priority.

"She's been so nice to you all year. She's let you come to class late, she's held onto your laptop for you, she let you get away with a whole lot of stuff until a week before Spring Break. Then she suddenly got mad at you and told you that you had to get your laptop from the office. And she won't let you be late without a note. Seems like she's mad at you."

I shook my head and tried to calm myself. Blake was not being mean or even nosy—he was just trying to sort out the facts. Facts that didn't make sense to him. "Yeah, she got mad about something I didn't do. She thinks I stole $50 from her when she asked me to get my laptop out of her car." I hated that she didn't believe me. Ms. Williams had really helped me at school up until that day.

"That makes sense," Blake stated as he looked out the window.

"No, it doesn't," I argued back. "She thinks I did something that I didn't do."

Blake turned his head to face me, but his eyes stayed focused on my backpack, which was on my lap. "But she has good reason to believe it was you. All the facts point to you."

"That doesn't make it true." I felt my face warm.

I had taken money that wasn't mine before, but not really stolen it. Like when people dropped money on the ground, I would pick it up instead of telling them. That was not the same as stealing. At least, I didn't think so. Those times I had been hungry were the times when I made every excuse that it was okay for me to take money that was lying around. Reality was that ever since I had been making money at work, I had less of a need to pocket loose bills. But the key point was that I had *not* taken Ms. Williams's money.

"Did you try to argue your case?" Blake asked, still staring at my bag.

"No," I answered. "I just kept going to class that whole next week, and then Spring Break started. I hope she'll just move on."

"That makes you look guilty," Blake pointed out. "If you didn't do it, and she's still mad at you, then not talking to her makes you look even more guilty."

"But," I started. Then I realized Blake had made a good point. "Okay, okay! I'll figure out how to talk to her. Maybe she'll believe me if I at least try." When Blake didn't respond, I added, "Are you happy now?"

Blake frowned. "Not sure why I should be happy." I rolled my eyes, but then he suddenly smiled, "But I *will* be happy if Ms. Williams stops being so upset in class. It will make class better for all of us. I like that she usually understands me, and I don't want to lose that."

I laughed out loud. "So, this is really about you?"

Blake's grin grew. "Of course."

"And Emma, right?" I had to tease him. Emma Tang-Lee was Blake's girlfriend. She was also in our history class and had always had an attitude toward me. But when she became curious about me, I shut her down because I didn't want her in my business.

Blake smiled. "Yes, of course, Emma too!" He looked out the window again as he added, "Seems like you two are finally getting along some."

I laughed, "I guess *some* is the right word." Emma lived near Aunt Clara's house, so it wasn't such a surprise that she ran into me at Oak Park one night. She shared her problems with me, even when I didn't ask her to. She said she was trying to be perfect but wasn't living up to her Asian American parents' expectations. Emma went on and on about not doing well on tests, not getting into a good college, and ending up in a dead-end job.

I really didn't get her at all, so I told her that I had to take life a day at a time. But it seemed she had to figure it out a whole lifetime at a time. We agreed that it sucked for both of us. But then Emma told me maybe we could find somewhere in between a day and a lifetime? Emma had been less angry lately—maybe she'd found that place. But I was *not* even close.

"*Some* is a good start," Blake said as he waved for me to start moving. It was time to get off the bus.

As we moved to the front of the bus, the bus driver turned his head and nodded at me. I hadn't noticed him when I got on the bus. I had just swiped my metro card and moved on. At that moment, my cheeks warmed. It was Pedro, the bus driver who had seen me at my worst the night before. "Good to see you're okay," the man said, but he wasn't smiling.

"Thank you." I swallowed but didn't say anything else as I followed Blake off the bus. I was thankful Blake hadn't heard Pedro speak to me. I was embarrassed. I was ashamed that the man had seen me at my worst. There was no way I'd let myself get that desperate again!

Chapter 17

Hillview Avenue

We walked along Hillview Avenue, and I was thankful it wasn't raining. Even though the row of six-story buildings did have a view of the city of Hancock, they were obviously public housing. A huge chain-link fence wrapped around one side of one of the buildings, creating a fenced-in courtyard with picnic tables and benches.

We entered Blake's building and began to climb the stairs. My heart started to race. Not because we were at Hancock's public housing, but because I was getting ready to talk to my cousin. I wanted to stay in this building for the rest of the week if I could. Hancock public housing offered me a place to feel safe.

And I badly needed to feel safe.

"You want me to wait for you in the stairwell?" Blake asked as we stopped at the third floor—he lived somewhere on the fourth floor.

"No, I'll be okay." I smiled. "I'll text you if I need you." I was thankful I had his number too. I'd never needed to use it, but he was part of

Ozzie's growing group of friends. Ozzie made me enter all his friends' numbers into my new phone. That was the only reason I also had Mateo's and Emma's numbers. Although, I didn't think they really saw me as a friend.

"Okay," Blake said as he turned and headed up to his floor. I waited for his stairwell door to slam before I dared to step into the third-floor hallway.

I could hear voices on the other sides of the doors I passed. A strong garlic smell filled the hall—my stomach growled. I had eaten my last granola bar at work, but the smell of any meal set off my insides. It was like a trick. It was hard to tell my stomach that it didn't mean the food was for me.

Rick Orem's apartment was at the end of the hall. I could hear a TV blasting through the door, which meant someone was home.

I took a deep breath and knocked.

Chapter 18

Steph Pritt

I knocked three more times before the door finally opened. "Hey, Lilly. What's up?" Steph Pritt, my cousin's current girlfriend, gave me a single nod. But she didn't open the door wider than her baby bump. She said the baby was Rick's, but I wasn't so sure. Rick had three other kids, all girls, with two other women. He was excited that Steph was carrying a boy, his first son. I guessed it would probably not be his last, either.

"Is Rick here?" I asked as calmly as possible.

"No. He's working." Steph suddenly looked down as her 2-year-old daughter, Nova, hugged her leg. She reached down and lifted the girl onto her hip. I smiled at the sweet little girl who tucked her face into her mother's armpit. Nova was not Rick's kid, and I had no idea who her daddy was. Didn't want to know, really.

"He has a job?" I asked, trying not to sound too surprised as I reached out and touched Nova's curly blond hair. She looked like a clone of her mother.

"Got some hours delivering for Hancock Pizza." She shifted Nova to her other side. "Look, Lilly, I got stuff to do. What do you want?"

"I need a place to stay," I stated as I grabbed the straps on my backpack and tried to sound as calm as I could. I would *not* beg, not now.

"Look! We don't have much room as it is, so there is no way we—"

"Just for the rest of the week," I interrupted her. I didn't want to hear about all the reasons why they couldn't help me. I took a deep breath, still trying not to sound desperate.

She began to shut the door as she stated, "You'll have to come back later when—"

"I'll pay you," I added before she could shut the door all the way.

As I expected, the door stopped moving. Steph quickly opened it all the way again and looked straight at me. "How much?"

"$200," I quickly offered.

Steph squinted her eyes and scrunched up her mouth. She took her time thinking. "$300."

I took a deep breath. $300 was a lot, but I needed a place to stay. Badly. "$250," I countered, hoping she didn't see me begin to sweat.

"Okay," she quickly answered. I felt my shoulders drop, and relief shot through my whole body. I guess Steph saw she had me where she wanted me because she quickly added, "But you have to help me with Nova when you're here."

"Deal," I answered without missing a beat. At that minute, I didn't care what else she asked for.

Steph smiled and then finally stepped out of the way of the door to let me into the small apartment. We stood in the kitchen area, and a small living room was right on the other side of the tiny kitchen bar. The couch had a laundry basket on it next to piles of neatly folded clothes.

A short hallway shot to the left, and I could see a bright red shower curtain through the bathroom door that was open at the end of the hall. On each side of the bathroom door were two more doors.

Steph walked me to the end of the hall and opened the door to the right, "You can drop your stuff in Nova's room. You can sleep on her floor or the couch. Your call."

I dropped my backpack next to the crib in the small room. There was a window that overlooked the I-238 Beltway. A fuzzy black rug covered most of the floor. I'd be okay with the fuzzy rug. Better than the concrete at the stadium or the wooden benches in the belly of the pirate ship. "This looks perfect," I said with a smile on my face.

Steph snorted, "You must be desperate!"

I felt my face warm, but I would NOT feel ashamed. Especially not in front of Steph. "You think Rick will be okay if I stay here?" I asked, not only to change the subject but because I needed to know if there was a chance I would still have to leave.

"Don't care what he thinks." Steph started to walk down the short hall toward the kitchen again. "It's my place, not his! As far as he's concerned, he's crashing here too!" She snorted again. "If he doesn't like it, then he can sleep somewhere else until you're gone."

My mouth dropped open. I thought it was Rick's place—he made me think it was his place. "Well . . . good," was all I could get out. I actually felt relief and suddenly smiled.

Steph started laughing. "Looks like you're in better hands than you thought you'd be, right?"

"I guess so," I answered, hoping that Steph was a better person than Aunt Clara had made me think she was. Aunt Clara always talked trash about every one of Rick's girlfriends, which really should have been a red flag. I didn't trust Aunt Clara with anything, so why did I trust what she said about others? I decided at that moment that I'd give Steph a chance to prove herself to me. But I wouldn't tell her that since she already seemed to be pretty tough. I just hoped it was a good tough.

"Here," Steph said as she handed me Nova. "You can start now. I got laundry to fold, and she keeps getting in the way."

I had no problem holding onto the little girl. If all I had to do was to keep Nova busy so Steph would think I wasn't a burden, then I'd do it. All that mattered was that I had a place to stay for the rest of the week. Besides, listening to the toddler laugh as I played with her let me escape. At least for a little while.

Chapter 19

Good

Steph hadn't been joking when she said that she didn't care what Rick thought. Because that night when I returned to the apartment after working at Hancock Burger, Rick wasn't too happy. They argued but left me out of it, even though I could hear everything. Rick didn't think they should take me in, but she told him it wasn't his call. Of course, Steph never told him about the $250 I promised her, so I didn't say a word.

Steph winked at me as Rick slammed their bedroom door. "And that's how it's done." She smiled, and that was it. I wasn't sure it was the best way to be in a relationship, but at that moment, it worked in my favor.

In fact, the rest of the week worked just as I had hoped. I slept at Steph's apartment and watched Nova during the times I was there and not working. I was even able to wash my clothes in the coin-operated laundry room on the basement floor.

By Wednesday, I felt myself settle in as much as I could settle in anywhere. It meant that I didn't have to worry from hour to hour or day to day, at least not for a little while.

At that moment, I felt good about my plan. Not great, but good.

I thought of my run-in with Rafi, Meg, and Nelson on Monday night. Rafi may have thought I was one of them, but he was clearly wrong! I knew what I was doing. I wanted to forget that night at the stadium. If my plans worked out, there wouldn't be any reason for me to ever run into them again. At least, that's what I hoped.

I heard my phone *quack*, so I picked it up off the floor next to my makeshift bed. Steph had grabbed extra blankets and sheets, and I managed to create a comfy space. It was almost 11 p.m., so Nova was already asleep. There was a second *quack* before I was even able to check the first text. It had to be Ozzie since he kept sending me pics and texts from his trip.

u still up?

I was right. A pic popped up with a view of Ozzie's new cowboy boots propped up on his living room couch.

LOL nice boots!

think i might wear them to school

u do u

Suddenly, another pic popped up with Ozzie giving me his best mean stare, but his eyes were still smiling. He was awful at pretending.

So, I sent him my best mean stare and then texted.

this is how its done

LOL

I was tired and needed to go to sleep.

ttyl. gn

WAIT!

Ozzie texted before I shut off my phone. Then a second text came through.

got a surprise for u

what? what is it?

not telling

but u started telling me

now u have something to look forward to on monday

now THAT'S mean!

LOL. ttyl. gn

And that was it; we were done texting. What in the world had Ozzie bought me? I sure hoped it was not a pair of cowboy boots. The last time anyone got me anything was last Christmas when I had stayed at Zonta's house for a few weeks. Her parents had bought me clothes, a nice blue jacket, and a red wool cap. The items meant something to me, and now they were stuck in the locker room. I hoped they would still be there.

But if Ozzie got me something that I liked or cared about, then it would be one more thing I would need to keep safe. I sure hoped it was something small. I could handle small.

Chapter 20

The Last Night

On Friday, I cashed my check for the week at Food Time Grocery and handed Steph $250 that afternoon. That left me with $10 from that week's check. I wouldn't get my Hancock Burger check until next Friday. I tried to shake off my disappointment that I hadn't been able to save money during Spring Break, but there was nothing I could do about it.

I didn't let myself worry about the next week until Sunday. I hoped that once I went to school in the morning, I could head right to my little locker room and unlatch the window. I hoped my stuff was still in the two lockers where I had shoved it, especially my warm blanket and the gifts the Joneses bought me.

I told myself that I'd be okay once I got back to school.

"I know tonight's my last night, but I just want to say thanks," I said to Steph as she made a second grilled cheese sandwich. I was chomping on the first one she had made as I leaned against the small bar. There were no stools, but I didn't care. Nova had already gone to sleep, and I was ready to head that way as well.

"If you want, it doesn't have to be your last night. You can pay me $250 every week," Steph smiled and flipped the second sandwich in the frying pan. "Nice having a built-in babysitter, and I can always use the extra cash."

I snorted, "I won't make enough money once I go back to school."

"But you work at Hancock Burger too," Steph challenged me as she removed the pan from the burner.

I took another bite, enjoying the warm cheese. As I chewed, I mumbled, "But that's only two hours at night, and I only work at Food Time Grocery on the weekends."

Steph looked up at the ceiling for a second, like she was adding up numbers in her head. "So that's still enough hours to make some money."

"But only $318," I blurted out, regretting it right away.

"So, you do have enough!" Steph smiled. "I think $250 is fair." She took a big bite of her sandwich.

I swallowed the food in my mouth and didn't take another bite. My cheeks began to warm. "But that only leaves me with a little over $60. That's not enough for food and laundry and metro cards and minutes for my phone and—"

"That's your problem, not mine." Steph shook her head. "Look, Lilly. I know you got it rough and all, but I'm opening up my home to you, so I think it's only fair."

I calmed myself down. I didn't want to say anything that would upset her or cause her to kick me out before the morning. "I really am thankful, but I already have plans for this week."

Steph raised her eyebrows. "Really?"

I forced a smile and answered, "Yes." Then I took my last bite of the sandwich.

"So, what are those plans?" Steph wasn't going to let it go. I held my finger up to let her know I needed to finish chewing, but I was clearly buying time. She put one hand on her hip and shook her head. "Really?"

As soon as I swallowed, I explained, "I have a place that I'm pretty sure I can stay tomorrow. If not, I'll let you know. I can always come back here. Right?" I didn't lie, but there was no way I could spend my time working only to pay Steph. Still, my answer was good enough for her since she just nodded and took a bite of her sandwich.

I hoped I could still use the locker room. If not, I could reach out to Zonta and her family since they were always willing to help out. But I wasn't ready to give up my freedom. As long as I was responsible for myself, then I could be the one to make the decisions I wanted to make. Even though the Joneses were nice, I didn't want anyone telling me what I should and shouldn't do.

Chapter 21

Happy

I never thought I'd be so excited to go back to school. That Monday morning, I climbed onto Blake's school bus and plopped down in the seat next to him. I'd stuffed my green camo backpack so full that it took up almost all the space between me and the seat in front of me. I'd left nothing behind.

"Looks like your plan worked," Blake stated.

"I already told you it was working," I snorted. We'd been together all week at Food Time Grocery, and I'd texted him the first night that I stayed with Steph.

"I know. So, why aren't you going to stay at Hillview Apartments?" Blake asked as he looked at the size of my backpack. "Because it looks like you packed to leave."

I suddenly felt my cheeks warm. Was I really that easy to read? "I haven't decided yet," I answered.

"Okay, good. You were so much happier at work, so I thought you might stay longer." Blake smiled and then looked away as he added, "You're more fun to be around when you're happy."

My mouth dropped open as I stared at the back of Blake's head. I *had* been happier, but that was only because I knew what was happening every day. But I also knew that I couldn't keep paying Steph. I was a little sad leaving Nova, but that was the way it was. I tried not to get too attached to people I stayed with because I never knew when I'd have to leave.

I leaned my head against the seat. I couldn't believe it even mattered to Blake that I was happy, or that he liked me better when I was happy. So weird. Nobody had ever said that to me before. I didn't even know how to respond, so I closed my eyes instead and let the noise of the chatter on the bus remind me that I was on my way to school. I was happy at school, and it seemed like my happiness mattered. At least to Blake.

But the fact was it mattered to more people than just Blake. I realized that a couple of weeks ago when I disappeared. I had left class when Ms. Williams accused me of stealing her money, and I hid out in my safe space—my locker room. I soon found out that Ozzie and Zonta were really upset and worried. But it was Mateo who found me in my safe space. At first, he had been pretty hard on me when he told me how worried the others were. Fussing at people was how I talked to people I cared for. But Mateo fussing at me didn't mean he cared for me; it only meant that he cared about Ozzie and Zonta.

Still, my happiness mattered to Ozzie and Zonta. It was strange but in a good way.

Chapter 22

Oh!

Blake and I made it to school with just enough time to get to first period. Although it seemed that being late to class wasn't going to be a big deal since there was still a line at a table in the hallway where prom tickets were on sale. Still, hurrying to class was not what I had hoped for since it meant I'd have to head to the locker room later. But I told myself that I had all day.

"Hey, Lilly." Ozzie smiled as I came through the door and walked right up to his desk at the front. "So, what do you think?" He stood up and showed me his cowboy boots.

"So, you thought you needed to add another inch to your 6'4" self?" I laughed. He was already a huge guy, but the heels on the boots made him tower over me even more. "Good you left your cowboy hat at home."

"Yeah." Ozzie smiled as he reached up and patted his Browns cap. "Not ready for that much change." We both laughed as Ozzie grabbed my backpack off my back. "Let me carry this for you."

The pack was slung over his shoulder before I even had a say. I frowned and laughed at the same time. "Okay . . . uh . . . so . . . what's gotten into you? They teach you cowboy manners or something?"

"Or something." Ozzie smiled down at me as he walked me across the room to my desk, which was all the way in the back. When I looked up at him and frowned, he said, "What? Can't I be nice?"

I shook my head, totally confused. "Okay, okay." When Ozzie placed the bag on the floor next to my desk, I did a dramatic curtsy and attempted a British accent. "Thank you, kind sir, for your good deed."

Ozzie laughed and bowed in return and attempted his own British accent, "You are welcome, my dear lady."

"Oh, will you two shut up!" Emma's voice made us both stand up straight and stare at her. Blake's girlfriend had her hair up in her favorite high ponytails with half of her dark hair still falling below her shoulders. The blue dye at the tip of her hair was beginning to fade. Emma's desk was in front of mine and had been all year. But at that moment, she was still standing up, and Blake was right behind her with a huge grin on his face. Emma suddenly laughed, "Just stop flirting and start dating!"

My mouth dropped and my face warmed. I suddenly looked up at Ozzie who looked at me. His eyes grew wide as he saw the confusion on my face, then he quickly glared at Emma. "Really?"

"What?" Emma looked between Ozzie and me and softened her attitude. "Hey, sorry, man. Not my business."

"That's right," Ozzie answered and looked at me awkwardly and almost growled, "I'll talk to you later." And then he headed back to his seat and flung his cap onto his desk.

I stared at Emma and asked, "What was that all about?"

Emma smiled at me and reached her arm out to Blake, who lifted her yellow duffle bag off his shoulder and placed it next to her desk. "I don't know, Lilly. You tell me."

I looked down at my backpack and back across the room to Ozzie, who glanced at me briefly before he looked away. "Oh!" was all I could say as my cheeks quickly turned red.

Emma snorted, "*Oh!* is right!"

Chapter 23

Shock

I didn't try to talk to Ozzie after Emma pointed out very bluntly that Ozzie really liked me. More than a friend. The fact was, I liked him too, and I had for a long time, but I didn't think Ozzie would ever like me, at least not in that way. So, I had pushed it out of my mind and hadn't allowed myself to even go there. He was an all-star football player that could have the pick of any girl in the school. I was shocked.

Once the shock wore off, I was worried. What if my reaction made Ozzie think I didn't like him back? I had just stood there like an idiot. But maybe he didn't think that. Maybe it was just in my head.

Suddenly, my stomach turned, and I remembered Ozzie's text to me about a surprise. What if telling me he liked me *was* his surprise? I kept hoping Ozzie would look back at me again so I could smile at him and show him that I liked him back. But he didn't.

But someone *was* staring at me. Mateo. His desk was right in front of Blake, who also sat in the back row. There was one desk between

Blake and me, but it was an empty desk since Carlos had been expelled for attacking Zonta.

Mateo usually never bothered to look back at me. In fact, he never bothered to look much at anybody or anything. Except, he was staring at me, holding one earbud in his hand. He didn't need to say anything—he just shook his head and turned to face Ms. Williams, who was starting class.

I had a hard time focusing during class and was very aware that my teacher avoided any eye contact with me. Still, she wasn't outright mean—she just pretended I wasn't there. I still needed to talk to her, but I wasn't sure when that would be. At that moment, she was not my priority.

I had an idea since Ms. Williams was ignoring me anyway. I pulled out my phone and sent Ozzie a text.

hey. u ok? can we talk?

As soon as I sent it, I wondered if I should have let him text first. I was new at this and felt totally lost. But what if I needed to say more? So, I texted again.

sorry emma ruined your surprise. thought it was really sweet

I couldn't tell if Ozzie checked his texts or not, but as soon as class was over, Ozzie headed out of the classroom so fast that I didn't get a chance to catch up with him. It looked like Zonta was right on his heels. Maybe he'd talk to her about this mess.

I felt someone touch me as I tried to head for the door. I turned around and saw Emma frowning. "Sorry," Emma said. "I can't believe Ozzie bolted out the door." She shook her head. "I thought I knew him better than that. He likes to joke and tease—guess I pushed the wrong button."

"That's for sure." I couldn't really be mad at Emma. A small part of me was relieved—I knew how Ozzie felt about me.

"I just thought you *both* liked each other," Emma stated. "I guess I was wrong."

I looked at her and frowned. "Wait, what do you mean?"

"Well, he clearly likes you, but you looked like it was news to you . . . like you don't like him the same way." Emma shifted her bag to her other shoulder. My stomach turned. I had been right—my reaction sent the wrong message.

"But . . . I do. I do like him . . . a lot." At least, I thought I still did. It had been a long time since I had allowed myself to think of Ozzie that way. I suddenly realized I had just told Emma how I felt about Ozzie. I didn't even think Emma was my friend, not the way Zonta was. Still, she was the only one there, *and* she was listening.

I remembered the cold night almost three months ago when Emma and I ran into each other. I had my huge warm blanket wrapped around me, even most of my face. Once we slammed into each other, I pulled the blanket the rest of the way over my head. I was so embarrassed. I didn't want anyone to see how I looked. I had left my jacket at Aunt

Clara's as I bolted out the door in my pjs, trying to stay out of the argument she and Kent were having. I wasn't sure who ran into me at first. But then, at school, she recognized my boots, the only part of me clearly visible outside of the blanket. At that point, I thought maybe Emma needed to stay out of my business more than anyone. She lived too close to me. I needed to keep her at a distance.

But at that moment, when we both stood there talking about Ozzie, I didn't care if she was in my business. I needed her to be in my business. I needed help figuring out how to fix things with Ozzie.

Emma's smile returned. "I knew I was right!" She put her arm through mine, and I let her. "So, you got to find a way to let him know you like him."

Liking Ozzie was something that I kept in the back of my thoughts, just a silly crush. I didn't have time, or even the ability, to have a boyfriend. I had so many other priorities. But suddenly, the possibility of dating Ozzie felt like a priority.

I nodded at Emma as I said, "Okay, I'll figure something out."

Emma smiled and whispered, "You got this."

I continued to nod—but I had no idea what I was doing. This teenage crush stuff was not me. It was too normal. I was nowhere near able to handle normal.

But still, it felt good, so I let myself smile as Emma squeezed my arm.

Chapter 24

Zonta

During our lunch break, I planned to go to the locker room to see if my stuff was still there and find a way to unlatch the window, but I decided I had to find Ozzie first in the lunchroom.

I spotted Zonta at her usual table closer to the large wall of windows that made up the far side of the lunchroom. Ozzie wasn't there yet, and neither were any of Zonta's other friends. I sometimes sat with them, but most of the time I sat with Vashon and his freshman friends. Sitting with them had always been a safety zone for me since they mostly left me alone. But at that moment, I needed Zonta. I hoped Zonta had been able to speak with Ozzie, so I headed her way.

"Hey, Lilly." Vashon waved at me as I began to walk past our usual table, holding my lunch tray. My backpack felt extra heavy, but I didn't want to stop since I had to speak with Zonta before anyone else showed up. "Got you some stuff Granny sent." He lifted a small brown bag and waved it at me. So I stopped.

"Listen, Vashon," I said as I went right up to my normal seat across from him but didn't sit down. "I've GOT to talk to Zonta. I'll come back as soon as I'm done with her. Okay?"

Vashon placed the bag on the table in front of me and smiled. "Okay, but if you don't come back before the lunch period is over, I'm going to eat what's in the bag."

I laughed. "I'll be back! Don't you dare touch my goodies from your granny!"

"Time is ticking," Vashon teased and then turned to talk to a friend on his other side.

I quickly reached Zonta's table and sat down across from her. I flung my bag on the floor, and I placed my tray full of mashed potatoes, meatloaf, and green beans on the table. "We need to talk."

"Lilly!" Zonta smiled. "Got so much to tell you about our beach trip." Zonta began to pull out her phone. "Took some cool pics—"

"About Ozzie," I growled as I looked around to make sure no one else was listening.

Zonta frowned, finally picking up on my desperation. "He's not here yet. Is everything okay? I saw him storm out of the classroom, but he wouldn't say anything to me."

"He likes me," I blurted out. "He like-likes me. Like a lot."

I expected Zonta to be shocked, but she just smiled. "I know. It's so sweet."

I stared at her for a second and frowned. "Why didn't you tell me before?"

"Because *he* wanted to tell you," Zonta said as a matter of fact. She leaned in and grinned, "So, how did he tell you?"

I felt my face warm again. "He didn't. Emma did." Then I told Zonta the whole story. "And I haven't been able to talk to him since. I hoped he would come to lunch with you, but he's still not here."

Zonta took a deep breath. "Well, I think he'll show up sometime. So just be calm, Lilly. You'll both figure this out. This is good stuff, not bad stuff."

I stared at Zonta for a moment. She was right. It had only been a few hours, and I knew we would talk to each other again soon. We had to. I pulled out my phone from the top of my backpack to see if he had answered my text, but there was nothing. I held it up to Zonta and whispered, "Nothing—not a word!"

"Give him time." Zonta smiled. "Trust me, Ozzie is really bad at texting." Zonta had dated Ozzie at the beginning of the school year, and it was a total mess. I didn't care, though, for two reasons. One, they were friends and probably always had been, and they should *never* have dated in the first place. And two, Ozzie had *never* been bad at texting me. I shook my head. Maybe that should have been my first clue that he liked me.

A few more friends sat down, and our conversation was quickly over. I excused myself to go sit with Vashon. My small brown bag from Mrs.

Wilkes was still where Vashon had left it. I opened it and pulled out four tightly wrapped homemade chocolate chip cookies. A small note was attached to it. *Sweet Lilly, I hope the rest of the year is a good one. In the middle of all your challenges, remember how strong you are. No one can take that away. Thinking of you. Mrs. Wilkes.*

My throat tightened, and I tried not to cry, but a couple of tears escaped. The last note sent to me was from Granny in middle school. I was so embarrassed that I tossed it in the trash. I couldn't even remember what it said, but I wished so badly that I had kept it.

"Yeah, Granny can do that to you," Vashon whispered.

I just nodded, folded the note, and tucked it into the small top pocket of my backpack.

I quickly ate the food on my tray, tucked the cookies into my backpack, and headed to the locker room. I had to get back on track.

Chapter 25

Locker Room

I only had a few minutes left before lunch period was over. My heart raced as I pushed down the handle of the little locker room that had become my safe place.

It was locked. A sick feeling crept over me. I slung my bag on the floor next to the door before I pushed down again, but the door still didn't budge. Suddenly, I felt a burning in my throat as the meatloaf began to come back up. I rushed to the nearest trashcan in the corner behind me and hurled up my lunch. With my head still over the trash can, I began to sob. How could I get my stuff? Where would I sleep? I was tired of making plans. Why couldn't I have just a little luck?

"Hey, you okay?" A deep voice and heavy breathing surprised me. I didn't look up right away since I suddenly realized I had made a scene in the back corner of the gym. I took a deep breath and slowly stood up, pushing my hair out of my face. I wiped my cheek with the back of my hand and hoped vomit wasn't in my hair.

In front of me stood Coach McCoy—Ozzie's football coach and one of my P.E. teachers. He mostly worked with the guys in the large freshman P.E. class. Coach Smith was our female P.E. teacher, but it was her first year teaching, and she always had that deer-in-the-headlights look. She knew who I was because I was the oddball girl taking freshman P.E. in my junior year in High School. I had failed P.E. at Hemby, and I needed the P.E. credit to graduate.

From the look on Coach McCoy's face, it seemed he wasn't quite sure who I was. But the facts that his normally pink, fleshy face was turning red and he was breathing harder than normal told me the heavy-set middle-aged man had moved faster than usual to reach me.

"Hi, Coach McCoy." I took another breath. "I'm fine. Lunch didn't sit well with me," I lied.

The man scratched his head and looked at me and then at the locker room door behind him, where my backpack was still on the floor next to the door. Then he looked back at me and frowned. "Come with me, Miss Orem." Clearly Coach McCoy *did* know me after all. He always called his P.E. students by their last names. His voice was no longer one filled with concern for my health. It had shifted. It was a different kind of concern that hit me hard. I knew that tone in his voice. It was the same voice he used when the freshmen boys decided to skip class one day.

My stomach turned as I grabbed my backpack and followed the man. Coach Mccoy didn't look back once as he walked to the other side of the gym, where the coach's office door stood wide open.

I could have kicked myself. I knew better than to head to the locker room without making sure the coach's office was empty, or at least the door and window blinds were shut. Stupid, desperate, dumb mistake!

Coach McCoy disappeared into his office, but before I was able to round the corner, his voice barked, "Coach Smith, I think I found the culprit."

Chapter 26
Guilty

I hesitated to step into Coach McCoy's office. Had Coach McCoy just said that I was *the culprit*? What did he mean? Why would he call me a culprit for anything? I was not a criminal. But if I didn't step into his office, I would definitely look guilty for something. So, I took a deep breath and stepped through the door.

Immediately, Coach Smith jumped up from behind her desk, which was set up along the far wall. She was as tall as Coach McCoy but about a third of his width. She ran her hands through her short brown hair, and her normally white cheeks were as red as mine. "Lilly, I thought it was you! But I hoped not."

"What's me?" I swallowed.

Coach Smith pointed at a pile of stuff next to her desk. My colorful, warm blanket was neatly folded with my blue winter jacket and red wool cap on top, and my black combat boots were placed next to them. A black plastic trash bag leaned up next to the pile, and I was pretty sure it was full of my extra clothes and all the other stuff I'd stored in the lockers.

I tried to keep my cool, but it was hard to pretend that it wasn't my stuff. I looked at Coach Smith, shook my head slowly, and said, "Not my stuff." I felt my voice crack, so I stopped talking.

"YOU'VE GOT TO BE KIDDING!" Coach McCoy's voice boomed. "Lie straight to our faces, Miss Orem." He plopped into his chair and leaned back. He folded his hands behind his head. "So, you don't think we saw you wear that coat and hat and THOSE damn boots every day during winter? I hate those boots—scuffing up our floor. But nooooo, I couldn't say anything because everyone wants to make sure you're okay. Coach Smith even has a pair of tennis shoes that you get to borrow every time you have P.E., and STILL, you lie to our faces! Then there's the fact that you take your morning shower in the girls' locker room most mornings. Coach Smith even makes sure you have a clean towel and soap. After all this school has done for you, you can't even tell us the truth!" I began to shake, and my throat was so tight that I thought I'd sob all over again. But I pushed myself to hold it together.

"Coach—" Coach Smith tried to interrupt, but Coach McCoy wasn't finished.

"So, Miss Orem . . ." He suddenly stood up, walked over to my pile, and picked up the red wool cap. "If this is NOT your stuff then you won't care if I throw it in the trash?" At this point, tears had escaped, and we all knew that he had won. He was right. I *was* a liar.

The man walked over to a trashcan next to his desk and dropped the red wool cap into it. The red wool cap Zeb Jones had bought me. One of the few things I owned. One of the few things that were a gift. I suddenly felt a part of me tear open—I leaped for the trash can and screamed, "NO!"

I pulled it out and ripped a piece of tape off it, the only thing that was really in the trash, along with a few wads of paper. "YES, IT IS MINE!" I waved at the pile next to Coach Smith's desk and kept yelling, "JUST BACK OFF!" I ran over to the pile and knelt next to it, shoving the cap into the plastic bag.

"What are you doing?" Coach Smith asked softly.

"I'm taking it all with me," I finally said without yelling.

"Lilly," Coach Smith reached out and touched my arm. I stopped packing my stuff into the plastic bag. "Have you been sleeping in the locker room?"

I paused and looked at Coach McCoy, who just stared at me, daring me to lie again. I nodded just once. But it was enough. Something happened. It was like a weight lifted, but that weight was filled with a total sense of panic. My lie was out, but I no longer had a plan. I suddenly found myself doing something I had never done before.

I begged.

"Please let me stay there. I promise you I won't lie about it. I always kept my stuff in the lockers. I never left a mess. I never broke anything or stole anything. I just need a place to sleep. Please . . . please."

By the time I finished begging, I was sobbing again. I had totally lost any sense of control and was so desperate that I didn't care about being ashamed or not. I threw my backpack down next to the pile on the floor. "This is all I have that matters—except one other thing I have hidden in a safe place. Otherwise, I have nothing." I looked up at my two coaches, who both had their hands over their mouths in disbelief. "There. You wanted the truth. Now you have it."

I sat down and rested my head on top of my stuff. I was so, so tired. I didn't even care what they said next. Nothing mattered anymore.

Chapter 27

Help

"Lilly." Coach Smith touched my shoulder, so I lifted my head. Coach McCoy was still standing next to the trashcan, watching me with a hand over his mouth. I guess I had shut him up. Coach Smith kept her hand on my shoulder as she spoke softly. "I think you need help."

At first, my own mouth dropped open. Did she really just tell me I needed help? Didn't she think I knew I needed help? Wasn't I looking for and finding help every day? Didn't I just beg them to let me stay in the locker room? I suddenly burst into laughter, but the laughter wasn't a joyful, fun laughter. It was a desperate, crazy, are-you-kidding-me laughter.

Coach Smith quickly removed her hand from my shoulder and raised her voice. "Lilly, stop it!" Her cheeks were red, and she kept glancing at Coach McCoy. Neither one of them knew what to do with me. I pulled myself together as much as I could and stared at her. It was my distant stare. That stare that I used when I needed to disconnect myself from whatever was happening. If I could go to that place, then maybe I could get through, maybe not the rest of the day, but the rest of that hour. I was back to making it hour to hour. Or had it narrowed down to minute by minute?

I should have stayed with Steph, where I had stretched my window of worry to week by week. Maybe it wasn't too late. I still had money that I had saved since I started working in January. It was the money that I hadn't used for my basic needs. Exactly $2,467 was wrapped tightly in a Food Time Grocery plastic bag shoved deep into a hole in Aunt Clara's couch. If I could just get that money, then I could use it for the extra things I needed and just give Steph the money I made during the week.

Then when summer came, I'd make more money, and *then* I'd make enough to save up again. It meant I wouldn't be able to use my saved money now for the thing I really wanted. I had planned on paying for my own place when I turned 18.

That was my ultimate plan. Make it until I was 18. That's what Granny had said, *18 and you are legally an adult.* I was so close. I couldn't believe how close I was.

"Lilly." Coach Smith started to shake me gently. "Are you listening?"

I frowned as I focused on the young coach's face, which didn't look much older than mine. Sometimes, I thought I even looked older or simply more tired. Had Coach Smith said something? "Sorry, no."

I heard Coach McCoy move before I saw him. He grunted as he knelt to my level. His body language and voice had changed. "Look, Miss Orem, I've radioed for help. You just stay right here. Okay?"

Radioed for help? What did he mean? Again, I didn't care much. I just nodded and laid my head back down on my stuff. MY stuff.

And they let me.

Chapter 28

3rd Period

3rd period P.E. started, and Coach McCoy told Coach Smith to stay with me while he managed the P.E. class on his own. I just kept resting my head on my pile of stuff. 3rd period . . . 3rd period?

I suddenly sat up. "I need to go to class," I stated as I got to my feet. "I can't miss Spanish."

"What? Wait. No!" Coach Smith reached the door before I even picked up my backpack. "You need to wait here until help arrives." She crossed her arms, letting me know she was not budging.

I shook my head as I lifted my pack onto my shoulders. "You don't understand. I can't miss Spanish. I need to be there . . . so people don't worry." When I said *people,* I really meant Ozzie, but that was none of her business. I hadn't seen him at lunch, but there was no way he would miss class. AND we actually sat next to each other in Spanish, so I *needed* to go.

"No, ma'am!" Coach Smith said as she crossed her arms in front of the door. "You are NOT leaving until help arrives. So, sit down and chill out!"

I was confused. "Don't you want me to go to class?" I pointed at my pile still next to her desk. "I'll come get my stuff after school since I know where I will stay tonight after all." As far as I was concerned, Steph was my best option. I'd pay her and still be in control, even if I didn't get to save enough money to pay for my own place yet. It could work—it had to.

Coach Smith's eyebrows rose. "Is that so? Then you can tell that to social services when they get here." Suddenly, her cheeks flared again. She hadn't meant to tell me who the *help* was that was coming, and I hadn't asked. I had hoped it was just the school counselor, but deep down, I knew that they had called the Department of Social Services. I'd dealt with DSS before and had hoped that I had outgrown the need to deal with them again.

"Well, damn!" was all I could say as I flung my backpack back on the floor and plopped back down next to my pile.

"Look, Lilly." Coach Smith dropped her guard position at the door and came to sit next to me on the floor. "We had to. You have serious needs that the school can't meet anymore." Tears began to fill her eyes.

"Please don't cry, Coach!" I shook my head. "I don't need you crying. I already feel bad enough having involved you. I should have never tried to get back into that locker room." I looked directly at her as she wiped the tears away, trying to pull herself together. I snorted, "If it makes you feel any better, this is not my first time with DSS. So, trust me, I got this."

Coach Smith frowned and shook her head at the same time. "It doesn't make me feel better, and I know you think you got it." Then she tilted her head as if she wasn't sure she should say anymore. She lifted both her hands and ran them through her short hair before she finally said, "But that's the problem, Lilly."

"What's the problem?" I was confused.

"You think you have got to have it all figured out. You think you have to have this crazy control over your life that no normal 17-year-old has. 17-year-olds don't have to worry about where they sleep or if they can get a shower." Then she pointed at my pile. "And 17-year-olds don't have to be afraid that everything they own will be lost. Not to mention, most teens could never carry all their belongings in two bags. Heck, they would have a hard time fitting half their closets into two bags."

I felt myself begin to slip again. That distant stare began to dull Coach Smith's words. Didn't she think I already knew this?

"Don't you dare slip away again," Coach Smith said as she slapped my leg. I felt a small sting through my black leggings. It startled me but didn't really hurt. I focused my eyes on my coach as she added, "I may not know much, Lilly, but I do know that you need to let people help you. You do NOT need to do this alone. You can't!"

I lifted my chin slightly to challenge her. "How do you know I can't?"

Coach's eyes locked with mine. "Because NOBODY can!"

Chapter 29

Wait

So, I waited. Coach Smith went back to her desk and pulled up her laptop. She was finally confident enough that I wouldn't try to leave.

My stomach growled, so I pulled out the four cookies from Mrs. Wilkes—thankful once again for her kindness. Then I checked my phone to see if Ozzie had finally texted me. I knew Coach Smith wouldn't care if I used my phone since it meant I would be doing something. Anything, really.

As soon as I saw I had missed messages, I felt relief. It was Ozzie. In fact, all of the messages were Ozzie's.

that wasn't the surprise

where r u?

r u ok?

plz tell me ur ok?

did u leave school?

sorry i took off in 1st period

emma messed w my head

plz come back to school

we need to talk

I knew he would worry about me. I knew it! I hated that he was worried again, but at the same time, I was relieved that he *was* worried—he had to still like me. I reread the texts several times. What did he mean that it wasn't the surprise? If letting me know he liked me was not the surprise, then what was the surprise?

I wondered if I should text him back since I didn't want him to get into trouble with our Spanish teacher. But I was pretty sure he had his phone on silent. I decided that it was probably best if I let him know I was okay, even if he didn't see my texts until after class.

hey

still @ school

stuck in P.E. office

in a little trouble cause i tried to get into locker room 2 get my stuff

school called DSS

not sure what's going 2 happen

sorry 2 freak u out

when i get through whatever this is i also want 2 talk

I read through what I had sent a couple of times and decided it was enough for now. I placed my phone on my belly and leaned back to look up at the ceiling. A couple of pencils were stuck into the white tiles, and I wondered if the coaches even knew they were there. I decided I wouldn't say a word.

Suddenly, my phone vibrated. I quickly picked it up and couldn't believe Ozzie had already texted me back.

omg r u ok?

I smiled and responded.

yes but it sux to have to talk to DSS

what will they do?

talk and decide what is best 4 me

that doesn't sound so bad

right, but i'd rather b in spanish w u

There was a sudden pause in our back and forth. Ozzie had to read between the lines, although I thought that the last text pretty much told him that I liked him too. He finally responded.

me too

I smiled and settled in for back-and-forth texting before DSS arrived. It was fun. It was what I needed. Ozzie didn't mention the surprise again, and I didn't push him. I was so happy we were talking. Any surprise could wait.

I was happy that neither one of us said anything else about the mess in first period. Ozzie told me he was able to text during 3rd period because they were working in groups on some special skit to show that they knew how to use specific Spanish phrases. He let his group take the lead, and he'd just do what they said at the end of class.

Letting others take the lead in a project was big for Ozzie because he always needed to be the one to make sure his project was perfect. It was something I had experienced with him, too, back in the fall when we had to work together on a project about the 9th Amendment. He wanted it to be perfect. Working on that project with him had caused a lot of pain, too, but I pushed those thoughts away.

After about fifteen minutes of back-and-forth texting about stuff that really didn't matter, I looked at Ozzie's latest text and my smile faded.

rmbr that night at 17th street café?

Of course, I remembered it! It seemed that talking about his current group project had also reminded Ozzie of our 9th Amendment project.

I really didn't want to text about it. I wanted to keep having fun—not talk about something serious. I had enough serious garbage going on right then. I needed to keep it light. I sat and thought about how to respond for so long that Ozzie's next text came through first.

sorry for bringing it up

I sighed. Now I had to say something. But what?

Chapter 30

That Night

don't b sorry

That was the best I could come up with in response to Ozzie's apology for bringing up the night we worked on a project at 17th Street Café. I wanted to say it was no big deal, but that would have been a huge lie. It had been a big deal in so many ways.

i am sorry. 4 all of it. needed to tell u that

I couldn't believe he wouldn't let it go. I needed to find a way to help him drop it, so I quickly texted back.

shouldn't we talk abt this in person? hard 2 text abt it

maybe. but im on a roll and don't want 2 hold back

I couldn't help but smile. He was trying not to run away from the uncomfortable topic—so different from how he acted that morning. I suddenly had to tease him.

is this ozzie texting?

I stared at my screen. Within moments, he responded.

LOL. seriously. i wished that night at 17th Street Café had never happened

Last fall had been awful on so many levels. But what made the project hard for me to pull off was that Ozzie thought we could just work on it like every other normal kid with access to a laptop and Wi-Fi at home. Something I didn't have! Ozzie hadn't wanted to meet me in person, but he finally agreed to meet me at 17th Street Café to work on the 9th Amendment project.

He was disgusted with my smell at first, but as we worked together, we actually connected. We both had fun discussing the amendment, and by the end there had been a breakthrough between us. But I hated that my smell bothered him. It suddenly became important to me to shower to show him that I didn't stink all the time.

I reread Ozzie's text over and over. We were clearly going to talk about it, so I finally responded.

im glad it DID happen

what? but u got hurt. because of me

That was true—the getting hurt part. I had gone back to Aunt Clara's that night and showered. Unfortunately, Kent showed up drunk and beat the hell out of me for no reason. I had grabbed my backpack and run out the door. That night, my swollen face and body hurt so bad as I headed to the closest gas station. As soon as the clerk saw me, she called 911.

2 reasons im glad

okay shoot

first zonta became my friend

When the ambulance showed up at the gas station that night, I handed the EMTs a little piece of paper I had tucked into the top of my backpack. It had Zonta's number scribbled on it. She had handed it to me on my first day at school. I thought she was too preppy and really too much, but I had held onto the piece of paper. Nobody had ever handed me their number to start a friendship. I didn't quite trust the fact that she so easily handed me her number. But I quickly learned that she had meant it.

In fact, she had an issue with being too nice all the time, even to people who were jerks. But she was getting better at setting boundaries. I was proud to be a part of helping her through her own garbage.

But that night, when I chose to call Zonta's number, I didn't know anything except that I needed a place to feel safe. The Jones family willingly took me in and made a home for me, at least for a while. I knew they would again, but I pushed that thought away. All that mattered was that night, Zonta became someone I could trust.

okay. that's true. so what about ur number 2 reason?

I smiled and didn't hesitate to respond.

because it was the first time i realized how much i like u

fr?

fr

I was so happy that we were way beyond that night. It felt so long ago.

looks like we have liked each other a long time

My cheeks warmed. I didn't believe him at all. There was no way he liked me then! So, I argued.

BUT u didn't like me then

i liked u. ur green eyes pulled me in. but then i talked myself out of liking u

My heart raced just a little. Could he really have started liking me at the same time? But I knew exactly why he talked himself out of liking me.

because i smelled

He paused for a moment before he texted back.

yes. and i hate myself 4 it

well. i did smell. so that was why i wanted to shower that night

As soon as I sent the text, I sent a second one.

i wanted u to know i didn't smell ALL the time

but it shouldn't have mattered

Ozzie was being very hard on himself. I needed him to know that I was not angry with him. It was not his fault that Kent beat me up. It was Kent's fault! But I didn't want to text those words. I wanted to keep it light.

but it does. that's life. i can't expect people not 2 move away from me if i stink

I hoped he saw that I wasn't saying it was right to be mean or hateful about someone who stinks. It is just a natural reaction to avoid bad smells. It's just that there had been, and at times still were, moments where I couldn't help that I stunk. I just learned to put up with the people's reactions.

u don't stink now

The relief I felt shocked me. I had just said it didn't matter, but it did matter to me as well. I was so happy he was gone during Spring Break, or else he may not have made that statement. The truth was that I had some odor issues then—only a week earlier. But he didn't need to know, so I kept it light.

LOL. i hope not

I also hoped that whatever plan DSS came up with would make things better. Not worse.

Chapter 31

DSS

"You have got to give me something to work with." Bev Bondy pulled her huge green cat-eye glasses off and rubbed the bridge of her nose. Her fake eyelashes closed and then slowly opened as she fixed her stare on me. "Lilly, let me help you!"

I stared at the woman who had tried to help me before. Many times. She had been my social worker when I lived in Hemby too. The only Department of Social Services building for Midway County sat across the street from Hancock's courthouse. I wanted to ask her if she was happy that she didn't have to travel as far to deal with me. Instead, I began to slowly swing back and forth in the swivel chair where I had been dropped off fifteen minutes earlier.

Coach Smith had quickly left me in the school's small conference room and closed the glass door behind her. I could see her speak with Bev Bondy, Principal Ketner, and our school counselor, Ms. Nazari. They may have been out of my earshot, but their body language told me all I needed to know. Hancock High didn't know what to do with me.

"I don't know what else you want me to say?" I said as I continued to swivel. My pile of stuff leaned up against the wall behind me.

"Tell me what your plans are." Bev slowly placed her glasses back on and pulled her long blond ponytail over her shoulder. She'd chosen a pale blond dye color that made her hair blend into her skin, so it looked like her forehead didn't stop. I wondered if Bev chose her large green glasses and unique look to let everyone feel a little more at ease. What better way to deal with DSS issues than to bring a little humor to the table. Literally.

"LILLY!" Bev raised her voice—she wouldn't let me slip into my own thoughts. As soon as she saw I was focused on her, she added, "Let's start with an easy question." When I didn't respond, she took a deep breath and asked, "How does your aunt feel about this?"

I frowned. "Feel about what?" I snorted. "Sleeping in a high school locker room or getting caught?"

Bev Bondy smiled just a little. She finally had me talking. "Okay, how about both?"

I held up one finger. "First of all, she didn't know where I was staying, and . . ." I popped another finger up. ". . . second, she doesn't know about me being caught, yet—unless you all called her. But even if she did know, she wouldn't care."

The long lashes flickered slightly. "Well, since you mentioned it, we did call her."

I shook my head. "I knew it."

"Look, Lilly." The social worker leaned in a little. "Ms. Nazari called your aunt right away. She had to! She's your legal guardian and responsible for you."

I laughed out loud. "Right!" I stopped swiveling and leaned in too. "Explain this to me, Bev—what is her responsibility?"

My social worker had told me I could call her by her first name when she first dealt with me almost four years earlier. At that time, Hemby Middle had called her when I was struggling to get to school and feed myself. I had welcomed Bev then. I just knew she would help me find another place to live—a place where people would care about me and want me.

Want me. I hadn't thought of those two words in a long time. It was one thing to feel safe, but it was a whole other thing to feel wanted.

But, no. She met with Aunt Clara, who promised her that she would get her act together. Bev had said that Aunt Clara just needed to learn how to take care of a young girl. I hated to admit it, but it had gotten better for a little while. As long as we lived in Hemby, Aunt Clara did the best she could to make sure there was food in the house. Even if it meant I needed to make it myself. Even if it still meant that I had to figure out everything else for myself.

I was fifteen when Bev told me, "Just because a parent or guardian is bad at parenting does *not* mean they are breaking the law. Not everyone can provide for kids like most middle-class Americans think they should. As long as you have food, clothing, and shelter and can get an education, then you will *not* be removed."

That had been it for me. Unless Aunt Clara hurt me in some way or another, DSS couldn't and wouldn't do anything. That was why Bev really got involved when Kent beat me up. She *finally* had what she needed to pull me out and find me a better place. But by then, I was done.

There was also the fact that the Jones family stepped in until Kent left Aunt Clara again—even though they had not been and still were not a foster family. If I wanted to stay there, then DSS would not push for a different placement. So, I didn't push. I was tired of pushing, and the Joneses were good people.

I had also seen relief in Bev's eyes that night when I said I'd stay with the Joneses. Because the raw-hard truth of it was that there were already more foster kids than there were foster families willing to take them. The last thing I needed that night was for Bev to struggle to find a place for me. The Jones family had made it easy for both of us.

"I know this is hard, Lilly." Bev took off her glasses again. "But your Aunt Clara is responsible for you. She signed a safety assessment plan last fall. It outlined all the things she promised to do to keep you safe. That not only included keeping Kent away, but she agreed to make sure you have a place to sleep and make sure to feed you and meet your basic needs."

"None of which she does," I pointed out very matter of fact.

"Any time I have come by to talk to her, she says you choose to stay somewhere else," Bev stated. "She has never kicked you out. She told Ms. Nazari that you just stayed with her son, Rick, and his girlfriend, Steph Pritt, last week." My stomach flipped. Although that was true, it was not like they had let me stay with them out of the goodness of their hearts. Neither Aunt Clara nor Ms. Nazari knew that I had paid Steph for that week, but I was over trying to explain myself.

But Bev had been right about one thing—I had decided where I would stay. That last month alone, I had slept in the school's locker room, at Oak Park, on Vashon's couch, and on the floor in Steph's daughter's room. Did that make my need to find a safe place to sleep *my* issue and not Aunt Clara's?

No, it couldn't have been my fault. The fact was that I hated being around Aunt Clara and Kent. That was the answer—Kent! "What about Kent? He's been back for a while, and I'm afraid he might hurt me again."

"Then why didn't you call me and tell me?" She shoved the glasses back on her nose. Her face began to turn red. "This means Clara did NOT follow through with her safety assessment plan! But how can I know unless you tell me? I told you I would help protect you, but you will NOT let me!"

Suddenly, I felt my own cheeks warm. She *had* said she'd protect me, and I *hadn't* called her. I looked down at my hands that were resting in my lap. It wasn't only that I hadn't called her since Kent came back, but

I hadn't even called her when Aunt Clara stopped feeding me. That awful week that Blake heard me yell at Rick in the stairwell. That was when it had all gone downhill, fast!

My throat began to hurt me. Was I really going to cry? Had the hell I'd been through since January been my fault?

Chapter 32

Adult

I stared at the conference room table. I focused on the sounds coming from Hancock High School's office just on the other side of the glass door. The ringing phone and muffled voices helped me pull myself together as best I could.

I couldn't look up at Bev Bondy. I was ashamed. I hated being ashamed. But it wasn't for being homeless, or for being poor, or even for stinking. I was ashamed that I had not reached out to her. I had given up on Bev right when she could have really done something. She could have intervened because Aunt Clara was violating the safety assessment plan that she had signed. It was something real. Something legally binding.

"Lilly, look at me." Bev used her best soft voice—one of her many voices. This was one that I liked and trusted. It always meant that she wasn't going to yell at me or lecture me. So, I looked up. "I don't know what's going through your head right now, but you need to know one thing." Bev took off her glasses and leaned in. Her thick eyelashes blinked once. "NONE of this is your fault."

My lips quivered as I argued, "But it is. If I had called you back in January, you would have finally been able to get me away from Aunt Clara. But . . ."

"But what?" Bev wanted me to finish my sentence.

"But now it's too late." I swallowed as I added, "I turn 18 next week."

Bev leaned back and returned her glasses to the bridge of her nose. "That's right. But the fault is still not yours. You did the best you could with the hand you were dealt." We stared at each other for a long moment. I needed her to say something, anything that would make me feel less helpless, less alone. She raised one finger as she added, "But that doesn't mean you're doomed."

"Doesn't it? You told me that when I turn 18, DSS can't do anything else to help me. I'm not a child anymore."

"That's not quite true." She shook her head. "DSS can't come in and remove you from a home, but you can get help in other ways—as an adult."

I sat up straighter. "How?"

Bev pulled a card out of the notebook in front of her. "I've told you about Ruth's Place before. There is someone I want you to talk to there."

"I told you before that Ruth's Place is for desperate homeless people!" I rolled my eyes. "I'm not one of them!" I pictured Rafi, Meg, and Nelson staying at Ruth's Place, and I was *not* one of them.

Bev frowned and tucked the card back into the notebook. "Do you really think you are better than they are?" Her eyes grew dark. "Desperate for a place to sleep in a school's gym locker room—you tell me how that's any different?"

"But I work and have a plan," I argued.

"Oh, you think every single one of the people you see struggling didn't have a plan or doesn't work?" Bev shook her head. "I'm really surprised, Lilly. You, of all people." She pointed at my pile of stuff behind me.

My cheeks warmed. She was right, and I hated that. "But I don't want to be one of them," I answered truthfully.

Bev nodded. "Okay, now that is more like it. Not wanting to be and pretending not to be are two different things."

"So, you think Ruth's Place can really help?" I asked.

"They work with DSS, and between the two of our programs, we can help with things that people need on a daily basis." Bev pulled the card out again.

"Are you able to help me with housing?" I asked as I only glanced at the card now sitting in front of me on the table.

Bev frowned slightly. "Not unless you were in the foster system, which you aren't. But we have programs you can be a part of to help you learn life skills."

I laughed, "Are you kidding me? I need a place to live. Now."

"You can still live with your aunt if you want to, or you can move in with the Jones family. I know they are still willing to take you in. But if you have another night with no place to go, then you can go to Ruth's Place for a few days."

I dropped my head again. "I know, but . . ."

"But what?" she pushed.

Still looking down I answered, "I can't have other adults thinking they are in charge of me. I don't need to deal with made-up rules that mean nothing to me—just remind me I'm in someone else's world. Not my own. I need to be on my own."

There was a long pause. Long enough for me to look up and see Bev's eyes widen. She had a look I had not seen on her before. Surprise. "Well, then," she said and gently smiled. "That explains a whole lot."

I frowned as I challenged her. "What is that supposed to mean?"

Bev still smiled as she leaned back in her chair. "It means that you feel you're an adult, but you're not allowed to be the adult you want to be."

This time, I was surprised. "Yes! That's right."

Bev leaned her head to the side as if she was thinking of the right thing to say. I had never seen her struggle to find the right words. But I waited. I needed her to help me make sense of the mess I was in. "Okay, you *are* an adult in many ways. You make sure you get yourself where you need to be. You work and have enough money for some of your basic needs, at least those Clara has failed to meet."

"I know." I was getting frustrated. I began to fold the card in two and then folded it again. It only took a few folds before it simply looked like trash.

"Listen, Lilly." Bev raised her voice just a little—that meant the lecture was coming. "But not having a place to live and being responsible for figuring it out is one of the hardest things that adults must deal with, even with full-time jobs. And everyone must follow rules wherever they go and whatever they do—especially in their jobs. Not to mention all the rules at school that you're already following—or mostly following. Trying to finish your junior year in high school at the same time is a stress beyond anything anyone can ever imagine."

"Again, I know this. You're not helping, Bev!" My throat was tightening again. I grabbed the now-ruined card she had given me and threw it in the trash. I was trying so hard not to cry.

"So know this: you decide," Bev stated. I was waiting for her to fuss at me for throwing the card away. But she didn't.

I looked over at her and frowned. "What do you mean?"

"You decide how you want to move forward. You decide if you want to put up with Clara and live with no rules. You decide if you want to check out what Ruth's Place has to offer and see how their rules fit your adult self. You can even decide if it's best to live with Rick and Steph, or you decide if you will take the Joneses up on their offer. Each place you go will have its own set of 'made-up' rules. But here's the thing—YOU decide. Then maybe you can be okay with where you end up and whatever rules are already in place. But you must think about what is important to you. You also must decide what will be best for you if you plan on completing a senior year at Hancock High."

I let the words sink in, but I was still confused. "How is this any different from what I'm already doing?"

"Right now, you're making hour-by-hour decisions based on panic and need, not based on logic and what is best for you."

It was like cold water had been poured over my head. A part of me woke up. That part that had been lying to me about everything being good hour by hour was suddenly shoved out of the way by a new part of me—part of me that I didn't know existed.

Could I really be in control and not just pretend to be?

I had to think that one through.

Chapter 33

Trespassing

"But what about today? What about the locker room and Aunt Clara?" I asked. We were moving forward with what I could decide as an adult, but we hadn't dealt with everything that had just happened.

"Hancock High will not press charges for trespassing—"

"Trespassing?" I was shocked. "I didn't trespass. I was just sleeping in my own High School's locker room."

"Which you broke into—"

"The lock was broken already," I corrected.

"Lilly," Bev raised her voice a little. "I said they will NOT press charges. You were in the school during hours when you should *not* have been, so let go of all your excuses—it was still not allowed." She was right, but I had painted myself such a great picture of how I was surviving that I made all sorts of excuses as to why it was okay—when it wasn't.

"And Aunt Clara?" I asked.

Bev looked at her phone and said, "Well, Ms. Nazari talked to her almost two hours ago, and she still has not shown up yet. So, I think she just might not show up."

"You think?" I teased.

"Let me check one more thing." Bev looked at her phone and shook her head. "Looks like your aunt texted an hour ago and said that the school called and that she isn't feeling well. *And* she asked me to find someone to drive you home. She also added that Kent is gone. I guess she knew that would be my question for her since she promised me that she'd keep him away from you."

I knew my aunt was busy kicking Kent out of her place before DSS showed up.

"So, *who's* taking me home?" I asked as I pointed at my pile of stuff on the floor behind me. "I have too much stuff to take the bus. I could use a ride. Unless the school wants me to stay for whatever is left of fourth period."

"I think they will be okay if you leave now." Bev smiled and stood up. "Give me a few minutes with the others." She pointed outside the glass door, and I knew she needed to talk things over with the principal and the school counselor.

While I waited, I looked over at the trash can. I could have pulled that card for Ruth's Place out and taken it with me. But I didn't. Instead, I quickly pulled out my phone and texted Ozzie.

headed home. ugh. wish me luck

Chapter 34

208 Maple Road

Ms. Nazari was assigned to take me home, but I was thankful that Bev sat in the passenger seat, willing to tag along. There wasn't much talk, except for Bev reminding me to call her if Kent shows up again. I promised her I would. It was the first time I meant it.

Before we pulled out of the school parking lot, Ms. Nazari looked back at me. "Lilly, I'm your contact at school should you need to talk about this or need something else." My school counselor's straight, jet-black hair curved around her light brown face, stopping at her perfect jawline. Bright red lipstick and matching, red-rimmed glasses, along with a well-fitting pantsuit, only made her look like she was a news reporter along for the ride. The fact was, she was very overdressed for 208 Maple Road. They both were.

I just nodded. Ms. Nazari waited a minute, but when I didn't say anything, she turned back around and began to drive. I knew she meant it—everyone meant it. But no one really understood. Bev Bondy came closest to understanding only because she had been on this ride with me longer than anyone else.

"Here we are," Bev stated twenty minutes later as we pulled up to Aunt Clara's house. Both women got out of the car and grabbed my stuff from the truck—they intended to walk me inside.

As I opened the front door, the familiar sour, musty smell hit me. The two ladies paused, but only for a second. The smell clearly bothered them, but I was used to it.

"There you are!" Aunt Clara got up off the couch with a sweater tightly wrapped around herself. Her dull brown hair was halfway pulled up in a messy bun—her attempt at looking presentable. "I've been so worried!" She lied as she walked over to me and tried to give me a hug.

I stood there and let the two strong women standing next to me take in the sad attempt. I just rolled my eyes as Bev gave me her best *just-chill-out* look.

"Where should we put her stuff?" Ms. Nazari asked.

My aunt gave up on hugging me and hurried over to the table that was shoved up against a wall. "You can put it all here. Lilly likes to keep her stuff right here. See how I left the space free for you?" I didn't respond as I nodded at the two women to leave my stuff on the empty table.

"So, where does Lilly sleep?" Ms. Nazari was checking every detail in the room as she walked toward the small area that acted as the kitchen. An old green fridge and a matching oven stood on opposites sides of a small sink and countertop. The only thing separating the kitchen from the living room was a small strip of linoleum that started where the wood floor stopped.

I looked at my aunt, who touched the back of the couch that she had been sitting on minutes ago. "She sleeps here." Then she smiled. "She said she thinks the couch is comfortable."

Ms. Nazari just nodded, clearly not happy with the answer. But it was what it was.

"Is Kent still allowed in this home?" Bev asked Aunt Clara directly.

She shook her head and answered, "Not anymore."

"You just ate dinner at Hancock Burger last week," I argued.

Aunt Clara smiled awkwardly. "Yes, but it's over now."

"Yeah, right!" I said as I plopped down on the couch. But they all ignored me as they stayed standing on the backside of the couch.

"You understand Lilly will call me if Kent returns." Bev's voice grew stern. She was not messing around.

"I do," my aunt answered. But she was just going through the motions. She knew DSS only had one week of any legal power over her. Because in a week, I'd be 18.

They talked about a few more things and began to head for the door. Bev walked over to me and leaned in close. She spoke one word. "Decide!"

I barely looked her in the eye as I nodded. She squeezed my shoulder before she left me alone.

My aunt walked them out the door and onto the small porch. There was a little more chatter, but it didn't matter to me.

None of it mattered. At all. Because I had decided.

As soon as they were gone, I would grab my money from where I hid it in the couch, grab my bags, and head out to stay with Steph. I had to. I didn't trust Aunt Clara for one minute. I never had, and I wasn't about to suddenly start—one week was not long enough to change anything.

Chapter 35

Gone

As I heard the car drive off, I flipped up the couch cushion and reached into the hole in the lining of the couch. I felt the springs and reached for the plastic bag on the other side of the deepest spring. I didn't feel it, so I grabbed my flashlight out of my backpack and bent over to get a look. My face touched the nasty lining of the couch as I shone the flashlight inside. There was nothing. It was gone.

Just then, I heard the front door close. Aunt Clara had just come back inside. She had finished talking to Ms. Nazari and Bev—pretending she cared about me. I sat back up and stared right at her.

Her eyes grew wide before she caught herself. "What's wrong, honey?"

"You took it," I said as I began to shake, a couch pillow clutched in one hand.

"Took what?" She walked over and looked at the mess I'd made of the couch cushions.

"You *know* what!" I practically growled as I flung the cushion onto the floor and pointed at the hole in the lining of the couch.

She gave me her best confused look. "No, I really don't."

I stood up and walked over to my aunt. She felt so small and weak. "You took all my money!" Suddenly, I made the connection. Something had felt so wrong when she had fed everyone at Hancock Burger, and now I knew why. "You used MY money to feed everyone. DIDN'T YOU?"

I had suspected she was dealing drugs, but I was wrong. She had stolen my money. At that moment, I wished she *had* been dealing drugs. If she had, then I'd still have my money.

I backed her up against the green fridge. The anger was so real that I saw fear in her eyes toward me—something I had never seen before. I quickly backed off. I was not Kent, and I was not going to hurt her. That was NOT me.

As I walked over to the couch and began to put the pillows back on, I felt a numbness crawl over me.

"I swear I didn't know it was yours," she said as she took a step away from the fridge. She was still on the linoleum side of the room.

I looked up at her and shook my head. "That is bull, and you know it! It was tightly wrapped in a Food Time Grocery bag, AND my paycheck stubs were still in the bag as well."

"Kent made me take it," Aunt Clara said as she took another step toward me, crossing onto the wood floor. "I didn't want to, but he told me you owed me for living here. That it was rent owed."

Rent owed—that was all I was, a renter. I was not surprised. I didn't think anything else that woman said or did could hurt me. I was wrong.

"That money was going to help me be able to live with Steph and pay her rent. Now you've ruined that!"

Aunt Clara's mouth dropped open. "You paid *her* rent? I thought you were just staying there." She crossed her arms. "So, you can pay Rick and Steph, but not me?"

I stared at her in shock. She had turned this around so quickly, making me the one in the wrong. I had no words. My anger grew, and all I could think about was Bev, so I grabbed my phone out of my backpack and called her. My aunt just stood and watched me, arms still crossed and a smirk on her face.

"Lilly? That was fast." Bev's voice calmed me some. "What's going on?"

"She stole my money! I had over $2000 stashed in the couch, and Aunt Clara took it and spent it!" I didn't try to hold back my tears. There was no way.

"You hid over $2000 in a couch?" Bev responded. It was not the response I expected.

"Yes." I frowned and wiped my face with the back of my hand. "Can you make her pay me back?"

"Lilly, you have no way to prove she stole your money. You *cannot* store money in a couch!" Bev was trying to use her soft voice on me, but all I could hear was a lecture coming on, so I raised my voice.

"DIDN'T YOU HEAR ME? She STOLE my money. I had nowhere else to put it!"

"A bank." Bev shot back. "You put lots of money in a bank. That's what banks are for."

I began to shake, but it didn't matter to Aunt Clara, who just stood there smirking at me. I needed to get away from her, so I ran out onto the front porch and slammed the door behind me. "Bev, I don't have a bank account. You know that I could never have let Aunt Clara open an account with me. She would have taken my money."

"She did anyway!" Bev was too direct. I wanted help, not directness.

"YOU'RE NOT HELPING!" I screamed into the phone, still shaking.

"Decide, Lilly," Bev said softly. "You have more control over your life and more help than you want to believe. Accept it. Believe it. And move on. As an adult."

I just sobbed into the phone. And Bev let me. She didn't tell Ms. Nazari to turn around and come back, but she did wait on the phone with me until I was done sobbing. When I began to pull myself together, Bev Bondy spoke one more time. "Do you think you can do this, Lilly? Or do you need me to come back? Because I will."

Bev's words soothed a part of me. She wasn't leaving me alone. She would come for me. I was still shaking, but my sobbing had given way to strained breathing. I needed to calm down. I took deep breaths until my breathing evened out some.

I hadn't even realized that so much of my panic was from that utter sense of abandonment. But Bev had not abandoned me. She was giving me an option—a choice. She would always be there for me. In fact, she had always been there for me, although I had not truly understood her role or her limitations. She had just reminded me that I was not alone. But that was what she had been saying all along, wasn't it?

I took one more deep breath as I finally answered, "Yes—yes, I can do this."

Bev was giving me the freedom to do the one thing I needed to do. Wanted to do.

Decide.

Chapter 36

Different

I walked back into the musty room for the last time. Aunt Clara was sitting on the couch and had the TV blaring. She had moved on. Like nothing had happened. I grabbed my backpack and the trash bags filled with my stuff and walked back out the door. Aunt Clara didn't even jump up and ask me what I was doing. Why would she? She had never cared before.

I decided to make the call I should have made in January. I should have decided to be with people who cared. Who wanted me. Even if it meant I had to figure out how to let others be in my business.

I decided to finally call the Jones family.

Zonta didn't waste a minute and drove over to get me.

As expected, her parents, Zeb and Monta were in tears when they came home from work and found me in my old room, the guest room. Zonta had called them before she picked me up, so it wasn't a surprise. Still, they embraced me like a long-lost child.

I wondered why I hadn't decided to do this earlier.

Why had it mattered so much to be in control when the more I tried, the less control I had?

I could figure this out—what all this complex family stuff looked like and what it felt like. Of all my choices, the Joneses were my best option. I remembered that the Jones family had rules that focused on forced time together. Like eating dinner together and letting people know where you always are. I found these rules strange the last time I lived with them. But maybe I could get used to them.

It was weird to step into their world again. It was different.

But I decided it was time for different.

Chapter 37

Monta and Zeb

I missed work that night. I hadn't even thought to call June and tell her I wouldn't be there to bus the tables at Hancock Burger. My stomach flipped—my boss was probably angry with me for leaving them one employee short. But when I thought about my whole day, I hoped that June would understand when I told her tomorrow. I pushed my guilt away and decided to focus on everything else that had happened that day. I'd deal with tomorrow when it came.

I texted Ozzie and Vashon to let them know where I was. I told them I'd fill them in at school since I was too tired to talk about it. They were both happy I was back with Zonta.

I was, too!

After I showered in my own bathroom, I climbed into the familiar bed—the bed and the bathroom I had chosen to leave in order to keep people out of my business when my only real business was surviving. I shook my head as I leaned back onto the soft pillows.

Suddenly, there was a knock on the door. "Lilly, are you still awake?" Monta's voice was soft and welcoming.

"Yes," I answered. "Come in."

The door slowly opened, and Zeb was standing behind Monta, peeking over her shoulder. "Can Zeb come in too?" Monta asked as she slowly stepped into my room.

My room. I had a room.

I laughed at the two adults, acting like I would run away if they did one little thing wrong. Of course, I had done just that, but it was not their fault. They had been perfectly normal parents, at least from what I had heard of the way parents were supposed to be. "Of course, come on in!"

Zeb quickly followed Monta, and they stood next to my bed as I sat up, leaned against the headboard, and stared at them. The fact that they were a biracial couple never really crossed my mind much. Not until I saw them standing next to each other that night. Zeb's pale white hand was wrapped around Monta's dark brown fingers. I had never put much thought into biracial couples before. But at that moment, looking at them made me think about what it might look like if I dated Ozzie. I smiled at the thought of Ozzie and looked forward to seeing him in the morning.

Zeb and Monta smiled back at me, thinking the smile was for them. Monta's smile was the biggest. "Lilly, we are so happy you're back."

"We really are," Zeb added. "But we want you to feel like this is your place."

"Like you have a say . . . like be in charge of your own—uh—choices," Monta quickly blurted.

"Zonta said something, didn't she." I laughed.

Monta and Zeb nodded, but it was Monta that explained. "We get it . . . well maybe not completely. But we want to learn more about what matters to you. We want you to feel like you can talk to us."

I smiled. "Thanks. I'm trying to figure it out too."

Zeb shifted and looked at Monta before she nodded at him to go ahead. He cleared his throat and said, "It may be too early, but we want you to have this." He pulled something out of his back pocket and placed it on my bed.

It was the phone. The phone that chased me away.

I reached for the phone and held it awkwardly. Had they kept the phone all these months? Had they hoped I would come back? I felt my throat tighten. But before I could say anything, Monta added, "It still has the tracker app—which we can take out if you want. You don't have to use the phone. In fact, you can just keep it here and then use it if you run out of minutes on your own phone. Or it can just sit here. Or we can—"

"Monta!" I stopped her rambling. "I will use it." I smiled. They wanted me to feel welcome and were even willing to remove the tracker app—willing to break one of their own rules of knowing where everyone was. It made no sense how hard they worked to make me feel at home. I had done nothing to earn their affection. But I didn't have to understand everything.

Taking the phone was the second decision I had made that night that would help me. If they really wanted me to use their phone on their phone plan, then I could let my other phone go and stop spending money on minutes. I could save money. And since all my savings were gone, I could start by accepting this simple kind act shown to me by Monta and Zeb.

Chapter 38

Sorry

Living with the Jones family again felt like I had never left. I was sure that was how they wanted me to feel. And I was thankful.

Even though it would be easy to fall back into the rhythm of riding to school with Zonta every morning, some things would take longer to get used to. It would be a while before my body stopped worrying about food, even though I had food available to me every day. All day.

It would also take time to adjust to not worrying about where I would sleep. That survival part of me would have to be reminded that I didn't have to pack my stuff and take it with me. It would take time to really believe that I would be back in the same bed that night and the next night.

But as I walked into school that Tuesday morning, I already felt a little more at peace. I was wearing my favorite blue sweater, although it was supposed to be warm that day. I also had on some fun, loose, pants with a wild hippie flower pattern on them. Monta pulled them out of her closet and asked me if I wanted them. Of course, I took them—they were fun and new.

I held my head up high as I walked into the school office and grabbed my computer from Mrs. Baker, who had it ready for me. I smiled at Mrs. Baker as I told her that I would be holding on to it now since I was living with the Joneses. She smiled and moved on to the next student waiting for her attention.

I believed it would be a good day as I left the office and headed toward my locker.

At least until Mateo came right up to me at my locker before first period started. He had his earbuds in his hand as he stared down at me. Frowning. "Where were you last night?"

I didn't know where to start with everything that happened to me the day before. I settled with short and to the point. "I had to find another place to sleep, so I missed work. Sorry."

"Sorry?" Mateo shook his head. He kept his voice low as he scanned the hall to make sure he wasn't drawing attention from others. "I had to cover your shift because there was no way I would leave June and Roy to pick up your slack. That meant I missed rehearsal last night. Thanks a lot, Lilly."

Mateo turned and walked away from me, shoving his earbuds back in his ears. I looked down the hall, but everyone was minding their own business—no one cared how red my face was.

But my embarrassment quickly turned to anger. How dare he!

I slammed my locker shut and walked right up to his locker. As soon as he saw me, he leaned against his locker and just crossed his arms. His earbuds were still in place, so I reached to grab one—but he beat me to it. "Don't touch." He held that earbud in one hand but left his other one in. "What do you want?"

I kept my voice down, but it felt like a quiet growl. "You have no idea what hell I've been through. All you care about is your stupid band." I took a breath as Mateo just shook his head at me. "You always judge me! What makes it worse is that you asked me to help you with your illegal immigrant girlfriend, but to you, I'm a worthless piece of—"

"Don't you talk about Alma like that." Mateo's face transformed to stone. "She wasn't my girlfriend. And we prefer the term undocumented. Get it right!" Mateo corrected me. He looked at me with disbelief. "In case you forgot—YOU are the one who told me to help her when her boyfriend was beating her. YOU were the one who told me I better do something about it. So, don't make this about how I've done *you* wrong."

Mateo was right, and I hated that. Just two weeks earlier, Mateo had found a way to get his Hispanic friend away from her abusive boyfriend. In fact, he had managed to get Ozzie, Emma, Blake, and Zonta to help with a plan. I had pushed him to figure something out because I recognized that she was being abused. But there was no way I could help her. I could hardly help myself.

But he knew that. He knew I had been sleeping in the locker room. He had found me there, but he hadn't told anyone. Did that mean he was protecting me? Or did it mean he didn't really care what happened to me?

"Then why are you so angry with me?" I challenged him. "And don't give me this bull about you having to cover my shift. You've been angry with me for a while."

Mateo looked at the earbud in his hand. Was he really thinking about whether he should answer me? He finally looked back at me. His voice softened. "I'm not angry with you, Lilly."

"Then what's up with all this *you-do-you* stuff you keep saying to me? Like you could care less?"

"That's the problem, Lilly. I do care." He looked straight at me. "I don't want to care. I hated caring about Alma, and it about killed me when she and her family left because they didn't feel safe here." I had heard that Alma and her family left town after Mateo helped her get away from her boyfriend. I could tell it had been hard on him and that he did care for her more than he let on.

"I'm sorry she left." My anger was suddenly gone. There were all sorts of other survival stories taking place outside of my own. It was hard for me to always see that other people could hurt, too, even those who seemed to have their lives together. Like Mateo, who was smart and had talent and confidence.

Mateo looked at the earbud in his hand. "I'm sorry she left too, but I know she will be better off wherever she ends up."

"But I'm not Alma," I stated. "I'm just doing the best I can with what I have."

Mateo looked back up at me and snorted. "So, riding the bus in the middle of the night in the pouring rain trying to find a place to sleep is doing your best?"

My mouth dropped. "How did you know—"

"Uncle Pedro drove that bus." Mateo shook his head. "He told my whole family about this white girl with intense green eyes carrying a camo-green backpack—a girl that was clearly struggling." Mateo pulled his other earbud out. "I knew exactly who he was talking about, especially when he added that you kept lying to him about where you needed to get off!"

My face turned red. That had only been a week earlier. He looked down at the earbuds for a second before he looked back up. "I worried that whole night about you and was relieved when you showed up the next day at work. But it is so hard to just watch you throw away your life—"

"I'm not throwing away—"

"Let me finish." Mateo didn't look away, so I shut my mouth as he continued, "You have friends and teachers who care about you, but you don't tell a single one of them the whole truth. You are the queen of half-truths! That IS throwing away your life, at least, your lifelines." He shook his head again. "And those people are now my friends too. So, I don't want to see them hurt by you."

I frowned. "But things are better now. Everyone knows about my couch surfing and issues with my aunt. I just moved in with Zonta's family, and I'm staying this time."

"Are you?" He asked as he shoved his earbuds back into his ears and headed toward our first-period classroom.

Chapter 39

Ms. Williams

As I followed Mateo into first period, I was pretty sure my cheeks were still red. But as soon as Ozzie saw me, he jumped out of his seat and came to walk with me to my desk on the other side of the room. I smiled at him, thankful my cheeks looked like I was blushing.

I filled him in on what happened the day before. It felt good to have someone listening instead of judging me. I didn't even look over at Mateo. I didn't want to see what his opinion was of Ozzie talking to me. Ozzie, who was now also his friend.

Ozzie and I avoided any liking-each-other subject—it didn't seem the right time or place to bring it up. But to be fair, I wasn't ready to talk about it either, even though I thought about it all the time.

"Lilly?" Ms. Williams suddenly stood next to Ozzie. My eyes widened as she continued, "Can we speak after class?" I just nodded as she smiled. "Good." Then she headed back up to the front of the class to begin.

"She smiled at you." Ozzie pointed out what I was thinking. "That has to be a good sign." He winked at me as he hurried back to his seat at the front.

"I hope so," I muttered under my breath.

At the end of first period, Ozzie waited for me as I packed up my stuff. I tried to smile as I walked toward him, and he shoved his Browns cap onto his head. Mateo was still sitting in his seat, gathering his stuff together. I was thankful he didn't see me glance at him. But his words had been bothering me all period. My lifelines. Friends and teachers who were my lifelines.

I walked right up to Ms. Williams's desk. She hadn't been as angry toward me during that class period, and I was sure Ms. Nazari had filled her in on all the drama in my life. Her explanation would have justified my actions as a desperate, homeless teen. I guess. But it would still have not been the truth. Not even a half-truth.

The fact was, I hadn't stolen her money.

"Ms. Williams?" My heart was racing, but I was in a better place than I had been in a long while. This woman was my favorite teacher—a real lifeline for most of the school year.

Ms. Williams looked up at me and smiled. "Great, Lilly. I need to talk to you about—"

"I need to talk to you too!" I blurted out. "I didn't steal your $50." I swallowed. "I want you to know I would never have done anything to hurt you. You have helped me more than any other adult at Hancock

High, and I would have been stupid to mess that up." I dropped my eyes briefly but looked back up. Ms. Williams opened her mouth to speak, but I quickly added, "But I am happy to give you $50 from my paycheck this week."

"Why would you do that if you didn't steal it?" She shook her head and shifted in her seat. "That makes no sense. Look, Lilly—"

"Because I want you to stop being angry with me," I interrupted again. "I have no way to prove my innocence. So, I might as well try to help make it right by giving you your lost money."

"Stop talking!" Ms. Williams raised her voice. "I've been trying to tell you that I found the money in my car last night."

"Oh." I stood there with my mouth wide open.

"I am sorry I blamed you. I feel awful about it." She turned and shuffled through the piles on her desk and pulled out a folder. "Here are your missed assignments. Get those in to me by the end of the semester, and you may just pass this course." She swallowed. "Take all the time you need."

I took the folder and didn't dare open it. Another thing I had lied to myself about. I told myself I had been passing. I came to class and did what I needed to in class. Surely that was enough. But up until the $50 disappeared, Ms. Williams had made sure I stayed on top of my missing work.

Looking at the folder, I realized she hadn't given up on me. But I still needed to do my part. I took a deep breath and nodded. "Okay. I'll have it to you as soon as I can."

She looked me up and down, taking in my clean clothes and washed hair, pulled back into two cute pigtails—thanks to Monta. My favorite teacher's warm smile was back. "You look like you're doing better."

"I am—" I started, then I dropped my eyes. That wasn't completely true. "I mean . . . I'm getting there." I looked up at her and nodded. "It will take a while, but I'm working on letting people . . . help me."

Ms. Williams reached out and squeezed my arm. "Okay, good."

When I turned to leave, Ozzie wasn't standing alone. Mateo stood next to him with one earbud in his hand. The looks on both their faces told me everything. They were relieved the drama between Ms. Williams and me was over.

Chapter 40

Lunch

"Where do you want to sit?" Ozzie asked me as we walked through the lunch line together. I was behind him and watched him grab two milks. He held them in one hand while he balanced his tray full of food in his other hand.

For most of the year, I had been sitting with Vashon and his freshman friends. Some days, I sat with Zonta and Ozzie—it all depended on what was going on. Vashon was always my safe choice. At that moment, I realized Ozzie had never asked me where I wanted to sit. It meant he planned on sitting wherever I sat. At least, that was what it felt like.

We both liked each other, so I guessed this was the first step to trying out what *liking-each-other* looked like. I shrugged and answered, "Where do you want to sit?"

Ozzie looked at me and teased, "I asked first."

I looked out across the lunchroom and saw that Zonta had a bunch of her other friends sitting with her. Summer, Imani, and Mary Ann were great girls, but I didn't know them well. Blake and Emma were sitting with them as well, along with Emma's best friend, Billy. There were just too many people. I glanced over at Vashon's table and felt drawn to it.

"I think I want to sit with Vashon." Then I glanced up at Ozzie and dared to ask, "Is that cool?"

Ozzie snorted, "No." But before I could say anything, he quickly added, "But I want to sit with you." Then he nodded toward the freshman boys and said, "So, let's sit with Vashon."

I laughed at Ozzie. He was trying hard to impress me with being flexible, even though sitting with Vashon was like sitting with his little brother, if he had one.

Of course, Vashon was so excited, as were his freshman buddies. They all were gamers, which made my life easier. I didn't have to pay attention to them, and they left me alone.

But Vashon was too excited when we sat with him. He didn't want to talk about video games. Not yet. "So, Ozzie, are you playing football next year?" Vashon pointed at his friends. "We've been taking bets on if you are or aren't." He grinned, but then his face got serious. "Not real bets—Granny would kill me. So, don't either of you tell her anything about it!"

I laughed at Vashon's fear of his granny. It was a good fear. But when I looked at Ozzie, he wasn't laughing. He adjusted his cap twice before he looked at me. I suddenly saw something I hadn't seen in him in a long time. Worry. Worry about something in his life. He always worried about others, but the worry I saw on his face was different.

Ozzie had torn his ACL at the end of last football season and hadn't been able to play for the state championship. The football team had still won without him, even though he was their star player. But the torn ACL forced Ozzie to deal with his own doubts about even wanting to play football anymore. It had always been his father's and older brother's dream, but Ozzie had the perfect build for a football career, and he had the talent. After he tore his ACL, his depression had hit him hard.

He also carried deep guilt for believing that it was his fault that Kent beat me up. Which, of course, was not his fault. It was Kent's fault. But Ozzie had also not stood up to his so-called friends who had said and done things he did not agree with, things that hurt others. As Ozzie fell into a deeper depression, he had planned to take his own life.

That was a day I would never forget. He had left hints telling us "goodbye," so we knew something was wrong and called 911. That afternoon, Zonta, Vashon, and I showed up at Ozzie's house after EMS had already arrived. We were relieved that Ozzie hadn't gone through with his plan.

His whole family had been in therapy since then. They promised him that playing football again would be his choice. Still, it was not a simple decision. Especially not a decision that freshman boys should be betting on. I suddenly wished we had chosen a different table.

But when Vashon saw Ozzie's face, his own smile faded quickly. Ozzie simply said, "Not cool, man. Not cool."

Vashon quickly answered, "Sorry." He looked at me and read my are-you-crazy glare. Vashon looked back at Ozzie. "Oh, man, I didn't think that one through."

"That's for sure," I answered for Ozzie. I looked down the table and saw no one was sitting at the other end. "Come on, Ozzie, let's scoot down a few seats."

Ozzie didn't say a word as we scooted down to the other end of the table. Vashon followed us, leaving his tray of food with his friends. Which was never a good idea. "Look, Ozzie, I'm so sorry."

Ozzie looked up at Vashon, who was standing next to him. He forced a smile and said, "I know you didn't mean anything by it. It really isn't such a big deal."

Vashon held his hand to his chest. "Thank God!" He smiled, but it quickly faded. "I really hope you do play ball again. At least for your senior year. You know you don't have to go for the pros. Just think about it." He paused, still looking at Ozzie, "But don't let your worries about what you'll do next keep you from enjoying what you can do now."

Both Ozzie and I stared at Vashon—had those words just come out of his mouth? I looked at Ozzie, and he was still staring at Vashon. But something had shifted in his eyes.

"What?" Vashon asked as he shifted to his other leg. "Did I say something wrong again?"

Ozzie shook his head. "No. That was something right."

Vashon smiled. "Oh, good."

"Let me ask you something." Ozzie crossed his arms and tilted his head up at Vashon.

"Okay, what?" Vashon looked at me for a clue, but I just shrugged.

"Did your granny teach you how to talk like that?"

Vashon's mouth dropped open. "Oh, no, did I just sound like Granny?"

"You sure did!" Ozzie teased. "But that's not a bad thing."

Chapter 41

Surprise

"Are you *really* okay?" I asked Ozzie as we sat alone at the end of the table. Vashon had returned to his friends and started yelling at them to give his food back. Vashon had quickly moved on.

"Yeah, I am. I really am." Ozzie pulled his cap off his head and placed it on the table before he grabbed one of his milks and began to open it. "I never thought of playing football in those terms. I think Vashon has a point."

I picked up my fork and shoved it into the pile of rice on my tray. "So, does that mean you might play next fall?"

Ozzie chugged down the whole milk before he looked at me and smiled. "I might."

"Great." I smiled back, but then something shifted in me. Next year. I hadn't thought much about my senior year since a part of me never really believed I'd do a senior year. The goal was age 18, and I'd reach that goal the next Monday. A part of me wondered what a year at

Hancock High would look like if I wasn't also trying to survive. But then, the other part of me needed to just get on with getting a job and finding a place to live once I could support myself.

"What are you thinking?" Ozzie asked as he dug into the rice on his tray.

"Nothing," I lied—then I remembered Mateo's words. "I mean, I'm thinking about next year." There. That was the truth—at least enough of it.

"How about we stop thinking about next year and think about right now?" Ozzie suggested. I nodded, very happy with the idea.

"Okay. Here and now," I said as I lifted another forkful of rice to my mouth. "I can live with that."

"Good." Ozzie opened his second milk. "Because I want to share my surprise with you." He rolled his eyes and added, "I wanted to yesterday, but you know how that went down."

"Yeah, let's not talk about yesterday." I looked at his hands and waited to see him pull out some silly gift from his trip to the Delgado Mountains. "Where's the surprise?"

"Will you go to prom with me?" He grinned as he held his milk halfway to his mouth.

I about choked on the rice in my mouth. I quickly grabbed my bottle of water and took a drink. Then I kept drinking longer than I needed to—I had to think about how I should answer.

"Are you okay?" Ozzie put down his milk.

I stopped drinking and finally looked at Ozzie. "Yes, I just got choked up. Sorry."

But Ozzie wasn't stupid—his smile was gone. "You don't want to go to the prom next week, do you?"

I took a deep breath. Truth. "Look, Ozzie. I've never thought about the prom before. How can I even afford to go?"

"Zonta and Monta already told me they would help out," Ozzie explained.

"But I just moved in." I frowned—it didn't make sense.

"They told me they would help out even before you moved in." Ozzie smiled. "They thought you would love the experience."

Experience? Was this all just an experience? Something to pull poor little Lilly into to give her a feeling of the privileged world? To see what she's been missing?

"Do you feel sorry for me? Did Zonta and Monta feel sorry for me?" I was beginning to feel like a charity case. I hated that feeling.

Ozzie frowned. "What? No."

But I couldn't hear anything else he said. I suddenly stood up, grabbed my backpack, left my lunch tray where it was, and walked out of the lunchroom.

Chapter 42

This

The first thing I felt when I stepped outside was the heat. Although it was still spring, summer's heat was already giving us a hint of what was to come. I quickly pulled my sweater off and looped it onto my backpack, then I started walking. I didn't care where I headed. Just away.

Was I only a charity case to Ozzie? Did Monta and Zeb feel like I was just some poor homeless kid they could help to feel better about themselves? Maybe I could just work more hours, live with Steph, and pay her until I made enough to live on my own. It wouldn't matter anyway if I didn't show up at school again. By the time Hancock High started asking questions, it would be next week. By then I'd be 18, and there wouldn't be anything they could do about my choice to drop out.

Drop out.

During the last two weeks of Granny's life, she had gently stroked my hair and said, "Whatever you do, don't drop out. Promise me?" I had promised her. But my promise to Granny seemed so long ago. Like it didn't really matter anymore.

I was done with this high school and all the stuff that came with it—crushes, proms, make-up work, grades, and trying to act like I was part of some normal life. I was not like anyone else—I would *never* be like everyone else. Bev Bondy was right that I had followed the school's rules—at least most of them. I had made it this far. But I just couldn't do it anymore.

I just let myself walk as I thought about my next steps. Suddenly, I stopped and paid attention to where I was. The football stadium rose in front of me. My stomach flipped. Why had I come back here? I should have been walking off campus. I looked at the space under the bleachers and was relieved to see no one was there. But there was still no way I was heading back under the bleachers. The fact was, I didn't know where to go, so I decided to head to the top of the bleachers. It was a pretty day, and I needed a moment to think things through.

I was out of breath when I got to the top, but it felt good to look down on the empty football field. A soft spring breeze cooled me down a little, but not enough to put my sweater back on.

I wondered if I should call Bev Bondy. Maybe she'd walk me through this. But she'd push me to talk to her contacts at Ruth's Place, and I still didn't think I needed that.

As I sat there thinking, I saw someone walking toward the bleachers. It was Ozzie. He'd followed me. But he stopped at the bottom of the bleachers, sat down on the lowest level, and looked up at me, waiting. He didn't wave or smile at me. Instead, he adjusted his Browns cap twice before he pulled out his phone and texted.

Suddenly my phone buzzed. I pulled it out but hesitated as I looked at the gift Monta and Zeb had given me—the new phone that I had accepted from them. A sign that I was buying into this picture-perfect idea of a family. But I knew that if it sounded too good to be true, then it probably was. How long before they were done with me, or I was done with them?

I finally read Ozzie's message.

r u okay?

no

I looked down at him, but he didn't look up me. Even though his cap hid his face I could tell he was focused on his phone texting me back.

y?

u feel sorry 4 me

I looked down at him as he looked up at me and shook his head. Then he texted again.

not true. y do you think that?

cause u want 2 take me 2 prom 2 have an experience. poor girl who needs 2 live a different life

I looked down at Ozzie, who was shaking his head as he read my text. I could see he was upset with what I was saying. But I didn't care. He asked, and I had told him. The truth. Isn't that what Mateo had pushed me to do? Ozzie looked up at me and held up his phone. He wanted me to see how he had responded.

did I say that?

I had to think a minute.

no. but i know it is true

it is NOT true. what can i say so u trust me?

i trust u

do u?

I had to stop and think. I looked down at him as he looked up at me. But I couldn't text him anymore. I had no answer for him. I wanted to trust him. I thought I did, but that fact was, I questioned everything he, or anyone else, did for me. A sudden burst of hopelessness hit me, and there was no way to stop the tears. So, I grabbed my sweater off my backpack and covered my head. I didn't want him to see me cry.

Suddenly I heard heavy breathing—Ozzie had sprinted up the bleachers. "Lilly, you don't have to trust me." He spoke softly. "Not yet."

I pulled the sweater off my face and wiped my eyes. "But I want to."

Ozzie smiled and sat down next to me, as close as he could possibly get. "Good. That's a start."

I took a deep breath, trying to calm myself down. As I looked out over the football field, I finally shared, "I just don't know if I can do this."

"*This* meaning us?" Ozzie's smile faded.

I looked at him as best I could through blurry eyes. "*This* meaning high school. All of it."

Chapter 43
Think About It

The 3rd period bell rang as Ozzie and I sat at the top of the bleachers in silence.

"You'll be late for Spanish," I said as I took a deep breath, trying to calm myself down. I'd been doing more crying than ever. I was so over the roller coaster ride I had been on.

"So will you," Ozzie stated.

"No, I'm not going." I stood up, and Ozzie quickly stood up next to me.

"Please, just finish the school day. That is all I'm asking." Ozzie looked down at the empty football field and then back at me. "It's like Vashon said—don't throw today away because of what you're afraid of will happen in the future."

I frowned. "That's *not* what he said."

Ozzie smiled. "Close enough." When I didn't respond, Ozzie added, "You've had a hell of a ride. But don't give up. Not yet. Please."

As I stared up at Ozzie, I could see something in his eyes that made my insides turn. In a good way. He meant it—not because he felt I was a charity case but because he really did care about me.

"I'll think about it." I smiled, just a little. "But I'm not going to prom."

Ozzie nodded. "Not a problem. I can't dance anyway.

Chapter 44

Awkward

I actually walked back into Hancock High with Ozzie and went to Spanish with him. The teacher was too busy trying to get his PowerPoint working to even care. He told us to sit down and leave him alone. I was thankful for the ease with which I settled into the seat next to Ozzie. Maybe I could do school. Maybe I could at least finish out my junior year.

The rest of the school day unfolded without any other drama. I headed back to Zonta's house with her after school, and we had a "family dinner" together at 6 p.m. There was a lot of chatter about the school day. I didn't bring up the fact that Ozzie had asked me to the prom and that I had said no. From the awkward looks Zonta gave her mother, I was pretty sure Ozzie had filled them in.

After a few more awkward looks, I rolled my eyes and said, "I'm sorry I don't want to go to the prom, but that doesn't mean you can't have fun getting Zonta all dressed up and stuff."

There was a moment of silence before Monta spoke. "I'm sorry, Lilly, if we made you uncomfortable. We thought it would be . . . well . . . we really didn't think it through. We should have talked to you first."

Ozzie had clearly told them *everything* I had said. I wasn't sure how to feel. I had never had people want to talk through stuff or even apologize to me. Who were these people? Was this good? Maybe. But would this last?

I gave them my best smile. "Thank you, but I'm fine. I'm just not used to—" I didn't even know how to explain it. I wasn't really sure myself. Do I tell them that I was not used to trusting people or that they were really too nice, so I didn't believe they meant any of it? There was no way I would say that. I didn't want to hurt them. They had been kind, even if I felt it was too good to be true.

". . . living with other people." Zonta finished the sentence for me.

I smiled at her and laughed a little. "Well, actually, I'm used to living with too many other people, just not used to staying in the same place without the expectation of leaving."

Monta reached her hand over and squeezed mine. "This is your home, Lilly, if you'll let it be."

The look on Monta's face made me uncomfortable. She sounded so dramatic, almost unreal. I wasn't sure she meant it. Still, I smiled and answered, "Thank you."

Chapter 45

Fired

Zonta dropped me off that night at Hancock Burger for my shift. She'd pick me up again at 10 p.m. It was only two hours, but those two hours still meant money. I hoped June would be okay that I missed the night before. I was thankful Zeb and Monta were okay with me keeping both jobs—at least, I assumed so since they hadn't said anything about it.

I walked into Hancock Burger like always and headed to the large storage closet and makeshift locker room for employees. I was proud of myself for being 15 minutes early. It felt weird not to carry my camo backpack, but I still needed to grab my apron so I was ready.

"Lilly?" Mateo stepped into the large storage closet with me. His eyes were wide, and he looked worried. "What are you doing here?"

I laughed. "I work here."

Mateo looked over his shoulder and back at me. "I'm not so sure that's true."

My mouth dropped. "What? But—"

"Lilly!" June Figby stepped through the door and halfway pushed Mateo to the side. Either that, or he quickly moved his body out of the way and up against the shelf behind him. His head seemed to be pressed up against a wall of stacked napkins. "Did you really decide to show up?"

I thought I knew what June looked like when she was angry, but I had been wrong. Her face was red, and she shoved her hands on her hips and stared at me, daring me to try to get passed her out the door. I could see Mateo was trying to figure out how to get around her, but he settled with staying where he was.

She was smaller than both Mateo and me, but she scared us both.

"I *am* sorry I missed yesterday. There was so much that happened, and I just—"

"I don't care," my boss interrupted. "You were a no-call, no-show."

"But—" I tried again.

"Did you not even think to call me to warn me that you wouldn't show up?" Her short, almost all-white hair seemed to be sticking out like horns through her hairnet instead of slicked back.

I looked at Mateo, who looked back at me, eyes still wide. I expected him to be excited to see me get chewed out. But he wasn't happy. He was really worried about me. About me? So, Mateo *had* cared about me and still did. Was he really trying to look out for me? His words about half-truths had really shaken me up, and I had been trying to break myself from the habit. I realized that at that moment, I wanted to show Mateo that I had been listening and I was really trying.

I suddenly didn't feel as afraid as I stood before my angry boss. She had a right to be angry with me. Not only had I broken a key on-the-job rule by not showing up, I had let her down—broken her trust.

"I didn't think of it at all." I looked June straight in the eyes. "My life fell apart yesterday, so work was the last thing on my mind." June opened her mouth to interrupt me, but I quickly added. "But that doesn't make it okay. My chaos shouldn't have thrown you and Hancock Burger into chaos." Stupid tears wanted to fall again, but I wouldn't let them, not this time. I didn't want June to feel sorry for me. Not June. She had always treated me like her employee, nothing more and nothing less.

My boss suddenly crossed her arms, still staring at me, but she didn't seem quite as mad. She finally said, "That's right." Then there was silence. I couldn't tell what she was thinking, but it still wasn't good. I had been a no-call, no-show, which meant I was fired.

When the silence went on too long, and Mateo's sweat began to drip onto his shirt, I nodded and swallowed. "I understand that I'm fired. Thanks for letting me work for you. I really have loved it." I turned away from my boss and hung my apron back up on the hook.

I expected her to make an exit, take Mateo with her, and leave me alone. But when I turned back around, they were still there. I took a step closer—but I couldn't get out unless she moved.

I shifted awkwardly. "Uh, I'm trying to leave . . . uh . . . but . . . uh—"

"Did I tell you to leave?" June held her chin up—I wished I hadn't gotten that close to her.

"No, but—"

"*No* is right." She dropped her arms and pointed that finger in my face. "Nobody is fired unless I say they're fired!"

Chapter 46

Something More

My cheeks grew warm as I looked at Mateo, but he just shrugged. It was at that moment that June suddenly seemed to realize Mateo was there. "Mateo," she half fussed. "Don't you have rehearsal to get to?"

"Yes—yes I do!" Mateo nodded, and June finally moved out of the doorway as Mateo hurried around her and out, leaving me alone to face my boss.

"So, I'm *not* fired?" I asked, really confused.

June took a deep breath for the first time, which put me at ease. I had never thought of June as another one of my lifelines, but she had been.

"Look, Lilly," she started as she sat down on a large box of supplies. "The fact is, I need you. You're a good worker, and you show up. At least until—well, you know." She patted the huge supply box she was sitting on. "Sit." I didn't question her. What June said, I did, so I quickly sat down next to her. She tucked the loose strands of hair under her hair net as she said, "You're family, you know."

I frowned and asked, "You mean like I'm part of the Hancock Burger family?"

June laughed and then looked at me. She was so close that I could see directly into her brown eyes with those flecks of green. "No, I mean family. Your grandmother was my half-sister."

My mouth dropped open as June's behavior began to make sense, especially how she pointed her finger at me, just like Granny. There had always been something about her. "Why didn't you say something?"

"I didn't know until your aunt showed up last week at Hancock Burger, and you were so upset. When you called her Aunt Clara, something rang a bell. I wasn't sure at first, so I spent some time digging. My sister, Fran, was born 13 years before me, but when her dad died in World War II, Fran's mother—our mother—remarried and had me. But Fran and I were so far apart in age, and she took off at age sixteen to do her own thing. I was only three. I saw her off and on. Fran never did marry, but I do remember when she had a baby and named her Clara. Our mother was so furious—we never saw Fran again after that. I guess Fran had another kid after Clara. Your mother."

"Who was even worse than Aunt Clara, from what I've heard about my mother." I looked up into my great aunt's face. It felt so weird talking about a past I shared with someone. "She died of a drug overdose when I was five—almost six—so I don't remember much about her, except that she had blond hair and a huge smile when she was happy. But she wasn't happy much."

"I'm sorry I didn't know," June said but didn't give me that look—that look of pity.

Before she had a chance to feel sorry for me, I added, "But Granny was great. She enrolled me in school the next fall since my mother hadn't even done that on time. Then she raised me until I was 14—when she died of cancer." My throat hurt me. "You remind me a lot of her."

June smiled. "I do?"

"You are strong like she was, and that finger . . . I knew I recognized that pointing finger!"

"Lilly, you are strong too, you know. The way you owned up to your mistake. That takes guts." June shifted on the box of supplies and crossed her arms again, but this time, it looked more like she was thinking.

"What now?" I asked, wondering what being related to June Figby could mean. Would she want to be with me?

June kept her arms crossed as she smiled at me. "You still have a job, as long as you don't let your chaos become my chaos."

It wasn't quite the answer I was looking for, although I was happy that I still had the job. What about the family part? Would June be the answer to all my problems? I took a deep breath and dared to ask, "Would you be able to take me on . . . to live with you?"

June looked at me and frowned. She dropped her arms, letting her hands slap her legs. "No way. I never had kids, never wanted kids, and there is no way I'm starting in my 70s!"

Crushed. I felt crushed. Why had I let myself have high hopes when we both just discovered we were family? Did I expect I would be a priority to someone else who shared my DNA? It had never happened with Aunt Clara. But June was different.

June reached over and grabbed my hand. Her rough skin felt strange. She had never touched me before. "I know you're disappointed. I get it. But I promise you one thing." She squeezed my hand. "I'll help you when you need me to."

I nodded. "Okay." Whatever that really meant, I had no idea. But it had to mean something. Something more than an hour earlier.

If nothing else came of it, at least I still had my job.

It was a good thing that I could do my job without thinking since all I could think about was what June had just said to me. During those two hours, my boss—my great aunt—would treat me like she always did when I worked my shift. She bossed me around and told me what tables needed bussing. Not for one moment did it feel any different than any other shift.

By the time I left, I forced myself to stop hoping for something that didn't exist. June was a great boss, and that needed to be good enough.

Chapter 47

Slow

I didn't say anything about June's news to Zonta or her family when I got back to their house. I focused on doing what I needed to do to get through the rest of the school year. Four more weeks of school until summer break, and then I'd decide what to do next.

I had a place to eat and sleep. I needed to be thankful and treat the Jones family the same way I did Mrs. Wilkes. Vashon's granny was amazing, and I was thankful. She set boundaries—I could stay with her again in an emergency. But that was all that she could offer. We had a clear understanding.

I had to think of the Jones family the same way. The way I saw it, we had an understanding. As long as I needed to, they would let me stay. I took a deep breath. Yes, I could work with that.

So, I did.

The rest of that week, Zonta drove us to school, and we talked about her boyfriend, Joseph. Emma Tang-Lee's brother and Zonta had become very close over the last few months. Joseph had helped her study for the SAT, and she had done well. Zonta went on and on about how Joseph had permission to take her to the prom—even as a freshman in college. He'd graduated from Hancock High the year before, so it was still okay. I was happy for them.

I worked hard on the make-up work the teachers had given me. Progress on Ms. Williams's file was slow, and passing Spanish was a long shot—still, I would try.

Family dinners were expected. I was thankful to eat something besides a burger and fries every night. There was always talk of the events of the day and plans for the next day.

After dinner, Zonta took me to work and picked me back up. The more we drove places together, the closer I felt to Zonta. She didn't have to drive me—I could have taken the bus, like always. But she wanted to spend time with me.

My time working at Hancock Burger didn't change. Nothing had changed there, except that Mateo stopped being so moody with me. He smiled and joked and told me how he and his band had been hired to play for Hancock High's prom. No wonder he had been so upset when he missed one of his rehearsals! I was happy for him too.

At lunch, Ozzie went back to sitting with Zonta, Emma, Blake, and all their friends. I sat with them once, and the other two times, I sat with Vashon. One of those times, Ozzie slowed down as he passed our table but then sped up to join Zonta's table. It was weird, but Ozzie was trying to give me space. When he sat down and glanced back at me, I smiled at him. He smiled back and then began talking to Blake. I wasn't sure what Ozzie and I were to each other anymore, but I was okay with taking it slow. Too much had happened too fast over the last two weeks, and I needed slow.

Chapter 48

Worth It

I welcomed spending most of Saturday at Food Time Grocery. It was the most normal part of my week. I understood what I was responsible for, and I was earning money with every item that I shoved onto the shelves. It was a familiar rhythm that helped me feel at peace.

Strangely enough, It was the only time that Blake and I lived in the same world without any of our friends from school. We didn't see each other much on Saturdays when we both were responsible for different sections in the store, but other times, we worked side by side. But it wasn't even about seeing each other. He and I both worked because we needed to, something that is hard to explain unless you have lived it. It seemed most teens earned money so they could buy what they wanted to buy. We worked to buy the things we needed. There was a difference.

"So, Lilly." Blake handed me a box to open. We were both working the canned vegetable aisle that day.

"Yes?" I cut open the box and pulled out canned tomatoes.

"Have you found out yet?" Blake asked. "You told me you would let me know when you found out."

With a can of tomatoes in each hand, I turned to face Blake, who was ripping open his own box of canned vegetables. "What are you talking about?"

Blake lifted a can of black beans out of the box as he answered me. "You know. You told me you would let me know when you found out if it was worth it or not." He looked up at me and then away again. "If it was worth being hungry and not asking for help. Remember?"

I did remember. He had asked me that over three months earlier. "That was a long time ago." I turned and put the cans on the shelf. "Why are you asking me now?"

"Because things look like they have changed for you." Blake shoved a can onto the shelf and turned to face me. "Now that you aren't hungry, I thought you might have an answer."

I stared at him, which, of course, made him look away. "Well, Blake, I haven't thought about it much." I slowly reached down to the box to grab more cans. Was it worth it? Had it been worth it? Blake just kept stocking the cans on the shelf, waiting for me to answer. I finally said, "I guess yes and no."

Blake stopped and faced me again. "That doesn't make sense. It is either yes OR no. Not both!"

I snorted. "I can *so* have both."

"Then explain," he stated as he grabbed another can of black beans.

"I liked making my own decisions—so that was the *yes* part." I waited a moment for Blake to respond, but he just stood there holding a can in his hand. So, I continued. "But being hungry and desperate all the time made it so NOT worth it."

"So . . . then it's a *no*." Blake turned back around to grab another can.

"No, it's both!" I argued. "I just explained it."

Blake frowned. "Not asking for help kept you hungry, right?" He glanced at me, waiting for my response. It wasn't that simple, but I still nodded. Blake looked at his can again and added, "So, even the decisions you made didn't help you. So, it is still a *no*—being hungry was not worth it since making your own decisions just made it worse!"

I sat there with my mouth open and watched Blake finally shove the can on the shelf. Then I shook my head and said, "I guess you're right." Then I smiled. "But believe it or not, I'm still making my own decisions. Just better ones."

Blake smiled back. "I do believe you. And it's about time!"

Chapter 49

Birthday

Monta had asked if she could throw me a birthday party that Sunday afternoon, but I had no idea she was going to go all out. The Joneses had a huge basement that she had decorated with balloons and streamers. The two brown leather couches that faced a huge flatscreen TV were filled with people. Zonta's friends, Summer, Imani, Mary Ann, and Billy, sat together on one, while Vashon and all his friends sat crammed on the second one. Ozzie, Mateo, Blake, Emma, and Joseph stood by a table filled with chips and sodas. A second table held a huge sheet cake that read, *Happy 18th Birthday Lilly!*

After they all sang "Happy Birthday," they had me blow out the candles that were shaped like the number 18. They handed out plates with huge pieces of birthday cake, which gave everyone something to do.

"Are you okay?" Zonta asked as she handed me my piece of cake. "You look like you're about to pass out."

I took the plate from Zonta. "I didn't expect so many people."

"You've got a lot of friends!" Zonta smiled and took a bite of her own piece of cake.

"These are *your* friends," I argued.

Zonta quickly swallowed. "No, no, no, NO!" She shook her head. "You are starting to sound like me a couple of months ago." She pointed at the pile of teens who had started to laugh and talk to each other. "These are not *only* my friends, well, except Joseph." She smiled at her boyfriend, who smiled back from across the room.

"But they *are*," I argued.

"Not true. You're friends with Ozzie, Emma, Mateo, and Blake. Right?"

"I guess so." I nodded. I hadn't much used the phrase *friends* when thinking about them, except Ozzie, but I guess they had become friends.

"Now, come on, Lilly," Zonta stated a little too dramatically. "I'm sure Vashon and all the guys you've been eating lunch with are your friends!"

It was true that Vashon had always been someone I considered a friend, but the rest of them? I guess, in a way, they had all been watching out for me. "Okay, but what about Summer, Imani, Mary Ann, and Billy?"

"Ah, those are your new friends. If you let them in." Zonta leaned into me. "I had to learn to make new friends. If I can do it, then so can you!"

I laughed out loud. "You're crazy!"

"What are sisters for?" Zonta answered as Monta yelled for her to help pass out more cake. As Zonta left me alone, her last statement hit me hard.

Sisters.

Why had she said that? Did she mean that? Or was it just a game?

"Aren't you going to eat your cake?" Ozzie grinned as he walked toward me, carrying something small in his hand.

"Yes, I am." I quickly took another bite. In fact, the cake was so good—best cake I had ever eaten. I wasn't sure I deserved any of this. Not the cake, not the friendships, and, for sure, not the pile of gifts I saw on a table at the foot of the steps.

"Good." Ozzie reached out and handed me a small piece of paper. "It's not much, but this is your birthday present from me." He dropped his eyes for a second and nodded toward the teens on the couches. "It's . . . uh . . . a private gift . . . nobody's business."

Private? I quickly put the rest of my cake down on a chair and took the envelope. "Okay, what is it?"

Ozzie leaned in and whispered, "Open it."

So, I did. There was a piece of paper that said. *This is good for one date with Ozzie Waxman, no questions asked*. I looked up at him as my cheeks warmed. "Are you asking me out on a date?"

"Sort of," Ozzie answered. "But I want to surprise you."

I looked down at the note and didn't know how to respond except to tease, "I'm sure I could make some good money if I sold this to one of your swooning fans."

"Very funny!" Ozzie laughed. But then we both became quiet. He reached out and touched the note. "Are you okay with this? Do you want to go out with me? See if you can trust me?"

There it was. He really wanted me to trust him. And I already did, but I hadn't given him a reason to believe me. I needed to give him one quickly, or else Ozzie might stop trying. I leaned into Ozzie and whispered, "Yes, I am okay and can't wait."

Ozzie's relief was visible as he let out a deep sigh. Had he really been so worried I'd reject him? But why shouldn't he be worried? I had done it once before.

As the party continued, I slowly allowed myself to soak up all the attention. It was a party celebrating me. Once I opened my gifts and people left, there was this strange quiet that filled the house. It was peaceful.

That night, I sat in my room and stared at the new clothes and a bright blue rolling suitcase that Monta and Zeb had bought for me, along with a silly wide-brimmed summer hat from Zonta. Next to the clothes sat a pile of gift cards I had received from almost everyone else.

I was in a strange place. This was not me. It could never really be me. One day it would all end, and I would be left with nothing *again*.

I had to protect myself before it was all torn away.

Chapter 50

Sick

"I'm sorry you feel sick today," Monta said as she touched my forehead. "It doesn't feel like you have a fever. But that doesn't mean you don't feel well. You probably just had too much cake last night."

"I'm sorry," I said and meant it. Not because I was really sick but because of what I was about to do. Again.

"Well, Zonta can bring back your missed schoolwork. You have our numbers, so if you need anything, just call Zeb or me at work, and we will be here in twenty minutes or less." The beautiful woman looked at me with concern and then moved in to gently kiss my forehead. But she stopped. I could tell she was trying to work on *not* being too intense, so she settled for a gentle pat on my leg. "Lock the door behind me and get back in bed. Okay?"

My throat hurt as I lied, "Okay."

As soon as the Joneses were gone, I grabbed my backpack and new suitcase and shoved all my stuff in them. The suitcase was easier to haul around than trash bags. It felt wrong to take my gifts and leave. But I pushed that feeling away. This was about survival. I told myself that leaving most of the gift cards would make it right. I couldn't buy stuff online anyway.

By 9 a.m., I was out the door and making my way along Bence Avenue toward the center of town.

I couldn't be hungry and desperate anymore. Bev and Blake had knocked that reality into my head. But I had finally decided to talk to people who could help me figure all this out. If I did it right, I might have a chance to stand on my own two feet one day.

Stand on my own two feet.

That was what I was counting on as I caught two different buses that took me to the corner of Winters Street and 3rd Avenue—to Ruth's Place.

Chapter 51
Ruth's Place

I didn't realize I would have to wait outside the large house. It was almost 10:30 by the time I reached Ruth's Place, but a sign on the solid wood door read *Doors Closed between 8:30 a.m. and 4:00 p.m.* The shelter was an old, one-story brick building that spread out on both sides of the front door. It felt like I was waiting outside of someone's home, a home that might have been some rich person's place back in the day. The only hint that there was more to the shelter was a second roof that rose above the original house. Ruth's Place had clearly added on a two-story building in the back.

I was sweating by the time I had pulled my new suitcase to a nearby bench. I didn't hesitate to lie down on the bench and prop my head up on my backpack. I could wait—I had nothing better to do. I just knew the people inside that building would help me. Bev Bondy had said so— she'd be proud of me.

"Look who it is: Green-Camo-Backpack-Girl." A familiar voice caused me to sit up very quickly. I was shocked to see Rafi standing in front of me. I didn't say anything, but I looked around him to see if Meg or Nelson were hanging out with him. "Nah, it's just you and me." Rafi answered the question I hadn't actually asked as he sat down next to me.

I scooted over and pulled my suitcase up next to me, but he didn't care as he reached down and felt the shiny blue material. "Looks like you've struck it rich."

"Don't touch it." I tried to pull it out of his reach. "And if I *had* struck it rich, I wouldn't be here, would I?"

Rafi moved his hand away and looked at me. "True. Then why are you here?"

"Why are *you* here?" I shot back at him.

The large Hispanic man pointed at the closed door. "I have an appointment with my case worker at 10:30."

"You live here?" I asked.

"I stay here when I don't have a place to stay, but live? Not sure if that is really living, but it keeps me safe from creeps. I don't like the thought of someone mugging me in the night. You know?"

My eyes were wide as I nodded. "Yeah." Of course, I didn't tell him that he was that person to me.

"Rafi?" Someone called his name from the door. Her black hair was pulled back in a tight ponytail that matched the tight look of her jeans and pink top. She smiled as soon as she saw Rafi and then said something to him in Spanish.

"Coming, Ms. Del Toro," Rafi yelled as he stood up. Before he left, he looked down at me and said, "You take care of yourself, Green-Camo-Backpack-Girl."

"Lilly," I said without thinking. "My name is Lilly."

Rafi smiled and then held out his hand. "Nice to meet you, Lilly."

I shook his hand and answered. "Nice to see you again, Rafi."

"Ah, you remember me." He grinned as he walked away. "I knew I was memorable."

I was surprised to find myself smiling as Rafi slipped through the door to speak to his case worker. Right before the door closed, Ms. Del Toro peeked out and took a good look at me before she closed it all the way.

I leaned back on the bench again. If Ruth's Place could help Rafi, then it had to be able to help me.

Chapter 52

Ms. Del Toro

"Excuse me," someone said as they gently shoved my shoulder. "Are you okay?"

It took me a moment to fully wake up. I hadn't planned on falling asleep. But it had been too hard to fight the warm sun and the fact that I was over-the-top tired. I quickly sat up as panic set in. I checked to make sure I still had my suitcase and felt relief as soon as I saw its bright blue color staring back at me.

"Hello." Ms. Del Toro stood in front of me. "You can't sleep here."

"Hi, I'm sorry." I shoved my hair behind my shoulders and tried to look more presentable. "I'm waiting for the shelter to open. I need to talk to someone." I pointed at all my stuff. "I need help figuring out my next steps. Oh, and Bev Bondy sent me." I thought adding that last bit might help convince her I wasn't just some random homeless person.

Ms. Del Toro's eyebrows lifted—Bev's name did matter! She looked at her phone and then back at me. "Well, I have a little time before my next appointment if you want to come in for a few minutes." She said it without any sign of sympathy or even concern.

"Oh, okay. Great." I jumped up, grabbed all my stuff, and followed the woman through the doors.

The entryway felt like we had walked into someone's home. The only sign that it wasn't was a bulletin board on the wall facing the door. It was full of brochures as well as a list of rules. "No Drugs" was written in bold. I followed Ms. Del Toro down a narrow hallway to the left and into the first room on the left. Two desks were squeezed into the small space. The caseworker slipped behind the one that had two extra chairs facing her desk. I quickly shoved my suitcase behind the chairs before sliding into the chair closest to the wall. I dropped the rest of my stuff on the floor.

As I sat across from Ms. Del Toro, it felt no different than sitting across from Bev Bondy or Ms. Nazari or any other person in the past four years that had tried to help me on some sort of level. A part of me had hoped that it would at least *feel* different. We went over my history and she took notes and nodded a whole lot.

After about twenty minutes, Ms. Del Toro looked up from her notepad and asked, "So, what is it you need, Ms. Orem?"

I pointed at my stuff on the floor behind me and answered, "A place to live and help to set up a bank account." Pretty simple, I thought.

Ms. Del Toro looked down at her notes and then back at me. "So, you're telling me that you had a place to live. *And* they were feeding you and getting you to school. Now you've suddenly decided to quit school, leave a perfect setup to come live in a shelter. A shelter where—" she paused and looked down at her notes, "—now that you're 18, you have to share a room on any given night with up to twenty other women?" She frowned. "I'm trying to understand this."

My cheeks warmed. The way she said it made me sound pathetic, unreasonable—almost stupid. "Bev Bondy told me to contact you and that you could help me with life skills. Like banking."

Ms. Del Toro leaned back in her seat and grabbed a handful of brochures off a shelf behind her. "Yes, I can help you find a program in the community that will help you learn to budget and open a bank account. But—" She looked at my stuff. "You don't have to live here to get that help."

"But I *want* to live here," I said with confidence.

The caseworker dropped the brochures on her desk without offering me any specific one. "You do realize this is NOT a permanent living situation," Ms. Del Toro said as a matter of fact. "*IF* you qualify to stay here, we will look at what your needs are and try to find a way for you to move out as soon as housing is available. But only when we see that you can hold down a full-time job and make rent payments. It usually takes up to 90 days for us to get a good idea of what is possible."

I nodded, trying to take it all in. Work full time. This was what I wanted. Live with up to twenty other women for 90 days. I could do that.

The woman across the desk from me sighed, "Why would you want to drop out of school and go through this process? Getting a high school degree is important. It will help you with job options in the future." She reached behind her desk to a different stack of papers and pulled out a single brochure. "If you really are going to go through with this, we strongly recommend these evening classes at Hancock Community College. They offer high school credit that will allow you to finish high school." This time, she handed me the brochure. And I took it.

I looked down at the brochure of three smiling faces, all holding a high school diploma. "At night?" I asked.

"Yes, if you can work days, then you can take classes at night. But IF you qualified, you would have to be back in the shelter no later than 10 p.m. Doors close at 10."

"But if doors close at 10, then I can't even keep the job I have right now at Hancock Burger. I don't get off until 10." I was trying to piece it all together. "I can't quit on June. She just let me keep my job after I was a no-call, no-show. I can't just leave her shorthanded again."

"Ms. Orem, we are *not* a free hotel where you can just come and go and do your own thing. We have tight rules. You already saw that we're closed during the day. And that's one of the easier rules to follow." Ms. Del Toro looked at me like she was beginning to figure something out about me. She tapped the notes she had taken as she added, "It seems you have some things that are already working for you. People who are already giving you the help that you need. People who are helping pave a path for you."

I frowned. What was Ms. Del Toro doing? Wasn't she supposed to welcome me into Ruth's Place with open arms? Why didn't she understand that I needed her help? Couldn't she bend some rules for me? I had to make her understand!

Chapter 53

Charity

I stared at the caseworker sitting across the desk from me. She would never understand me if I wasn't completely honest with her. But, before I could say anything, Ms. Del Toro tapped her notes and said, "I think the Joneses are still a good fit for you."

"But I don't want their charity. I don't want the Joneses to take me in because they feel sorry for me." It was the truth—it was the way I felt, and it had to count for something.

Ms. Del Toro's mouth dropped open for one second before she suddenly laughed. "And staying in a homeless shelter is not charity?" My cheeks warmed again. But Ms. Del Toro was not finished. "Look, Ms. Orem, funding for our shelter, for all that you see and all that you don't see, comes from people who feel sorry for homeless people. Every one of us here needs people to care about other people who have very little."

"But I have very little." I pointed at the pile of stuff behind me. Bev Bondy's lectures were nothing compared to Ms. Del Toro's.

The caseworker shook her head. "When I say little, I do not mean *things*. I mean support systems and resources. We need people to care about the teens who run away from their homes. Maybe they are pregnant, or their families don't accept them. They run to us in fear and have no idea what their next steps are."

I shifted in my seat. "Okay, but—"

She wasn't finished. "We need people to care about the single parent. Some can't feed their kids. Others have no place to stay except their car, or they sleep in a tent in a park. Forget being able to hold down a job—they just can't. We need people who will give money and support us because they care."

My throat hurt me. I was on the edge of tears. "I didn't mean—"

"Look, Ms. Orem." Ms. Del Toro stopped me before I could try to explain myself. "We are set up to help people who have no support—no resources." She shook her head and pointed at her notes again. "And you already have them. A family that wants you. A job on the weekend *and* a night job. One you don't want to leave because it's clearly a place you feel supported. Then there is Hancock High, which still wants to do its part to help you. All this means that you *DO NOT* qualify to live here. The beds here are for people who have no safe place to go. And that is *not* you!"

Chapter 54

We

It was too much for me to take in. I came to Ruth's Place to feel heard. I thought Ms. Del Toro would help me, but she was just flipping my world on its head all over again. I had no words. All I could do was give in to the hurt in my throat and cry. And I hated that.

So, I cried and cried, and all Ms. Del Toro did was hand me a tissue box. At one point, I sobbed, "But you helped Rafi."

Ms. Del Toro's voice softened a little. "I can't talk about anybody else. But I can tell you that everyone's story is different."

I shook my head. "That doesn't help me understand why he can get help and I can't."

The case worker took a deep breath. "I can tell you one thing. You have something in common with a lot of the people who seek us out."

I looked up at her as I grabbed a tissue from the box. "I do?"

"You are all survivors." She pointed at that notepad again. "Except you have more resources than most."

"But my story is awful too." I blew my nose.

"Yes, it is." Ms. Del Toro stood up and walked over to me for the first time. She sat down in the empty chair next to me as she continued, "We all have our stories. No one's story is better or worse because, for each one of us, our own story *is* the worst story." She leaned in and added, "But each one of us has to look at our story and embrace it as ours."

"What do you mean?" I had stopped crying.

Ms. Del Toro finally gave me that smile that she had given Rafi. "You must be proud of how you see the world differently. You can't be ashamed of it because it has formed you into who you are. BUT if you're wise," she paused and looked me right in the eye, "this part is the hard part, so listen." I nodded. "If you are wise, you will recognize the strengths not only in yourself but in those who care for you. Recognize them and THEN accept them at face value."

It was like Ms. Del Toro was eating away at that part of me that I hated. That part of me that could take charity from others but never quite trust their intention. "But how do I do that?"

"Don't read between the lines when there might not be anything wrong! Don't expect the worst and then sabotage a good situation because you *think* it will get bad. You have to start to question why you don't trust someone. Are the rules *really* the problem? What made you feel the way you do? Are those feelings telling you the truth or not?

Often, they are not, but we have been hurt so many times that we can't even see the truth and goodness when it stands in front of us."

"You keep saying *we*?" I stated.

"Yes, I was in the same situation as you. I was one of those teens that walked through those doors many years ago. Ruth's Place helped me find my way back from a dark place." She smiled. "But I didn't have your resources or support group. Once I did, and I believed it was the real deal, then I was able to soar."

I glanced at the notepad still sitting on her desk. "So, you think I have the real deal?"

She smiled again as she said, "I do, but it doesn't really matter what I think." The caseworker sighed again. "My caseworker put a lot of time and energy into helping me understand what I could and couldn't control. That Bev Bondy was something else!"

My mouth dropped open. "Bev was your caseworker?" Ms. Del Toro just nodded. Now it all made sense. I remembered the card Bev had given me—the card I had thrown in the trash. "Bev didn't want me to come here to live here, did she? She wanted me to talk to you!"

Ms. Del Toro laughed. "You never know with her, but I think that is a pretty good guess!" Then the case worker looked at my stuff. "Are you beginning to see that you have a good start to make it out there without taking up one of our beds?"

For a second, I believed her. For a second, I felt hope. There were my teachers—they helped me make up the work I needed to pass my courses. I had two jobs that mattered to me, and I seemed to matter to my bosses. And then there was Ozzie, who really cared about me, even though it didn't make sense to me. Even Blake, Mateo, and Emma were becoming friends. I remembered Vashon and his granny. Mrs. Wilkes had even sent me cookies and a note, which was still tucked in my backpack—a note reminding me of my strength. Even she believed in me. Then there were the Joneses, who really wanted to help. Except I still didn't see why they cared so much.

Then my hope vanished. "But I left." I suddenly felt sick. "Zeb and Monta will be so upset. They'll never take me back!"

"You don't *really* know that, do you?" Ms. Del Toro stated.

Truth. What was the truth?

"No, I don't," I answered. Suddenly, I felt a flicker of hope.

Chapter 55

Trust

There was a sudden knocking on the front door, followed by the sound of a ringing doorbell. The knocking and the ringing wouldn't let up. Ms. Del Toro frowned, "Stay here. Sometimes people hope to get into the shelter earlier."

I did as she told me to and sat in the office as the knocking and ringing continued. Suddenly, I heard loud voices, which quickly became quiet. When Ms. Del Toro didn't return right away, I got up out of my seat and went to the office door. The caseworker had left it cracked open. I was close enough to hear Ms. Del Toro say, "You will have to speak with her."

Was she talking about me?

A male responded, "But how can I get her to trust me? To trust us?"

I knew that voice. It was Zeb. How had he found me? I began to shake as I thought about what I could say to explain my actions. Ms. Del

Toro continued, "Look, Mr. Jones, I don't have the perfect answer. People like Lilly take a long time to really trust someone."

People like me? Sure, I had an issue with trust, but did I fit into some group? The people-who-don't-trust group? I felt my cheeks warm. How dare Ms. Del Toro say that about me! I knew how to trust. I just didn't think—

"That's not good enough." Zeb's response shut down my runaway thoughts. "Monta and I have tried to show her that we care about her and that she can trust us. We want her to trust us. Please tell me something—anything that will help. Please!"

My mouth dropped open. Zeb and Monta *really* cared about me— had I been so wrong about them? Had they not just been kind out of charity?

"First of all, you need to understand one thing. *Not trusting* has been a survival tool," Ms. Del Toro said a little louder than she needed to.

"What do you mean?" Zeb asked.

Ms. Del Toro explained, "For people like Lilly, the concept—the idea of trust—is really hard to understand because there really have not been many people to trust. There is a good chance that any real feeling of trust has been met with hurt. For example, you trust that you'll have a safe place to sleep, and then suddenly, you're attacked by someone in your home. You quickly learn to not trust that person. You remove yourself from them so you will not be attacked again. So, *not trusting* means keeping yourself safe."

For people like me? She had said it again. But this time, it felt different. She was right. I *had* learned to keep myself safe by not trusting others—at least not fully trusting them.

I remembered Emma and Mateo calling me out for my half-truths. They had been right. I thought I was protecting myself. But I had only pushed others away—others who I should have dared to trust.

"But she *is* safe with us!" Zeb sounded frustrated. "How can I get her to believe it?"

"Keep loving her," Ms. Del Toro said. "You keep showing her you care, and then maybe, one day, she will believe you mean it."

"How will I know?" Zeb's asked.

"When she dares to act like every other teen," Ms. Del Toro said even louder. I rolled my eyes—she was clearly not *only* talking to Zeb. She added, "When she's arguing and fussing and fighting with you, like your own child, *without* running away—then you'll know."

I leaned my head against the door frame. Once again, this woman who barely knew me was right. I thought I acted like every other teen, but I had only been fooling myself. I remembered Coach Smith telling me that 17-year-olds don't need to carry all their stuff with them or worry about where they will sleep or shower. She'd also said that I couldn't do it all alone—not because I was weak, but because nobody could.

I hadn't realized until that moment that maybe Zeb, Monta, and Zonta were my shot at not being alone anymore. But I hadn't let Zeb and Monta know my fears or even been real with them about much at all. I had really messed up a chance with them. I never thought they'd want me back, not after what I had done to them not once, but twice.

"Are you ready to speak with her?" Ms. Del Toro asked Zeb.

I held my breath as I waited for him to answer. "Do you think she will want to talk to me?" he asked.

Ms. Del Toro answered, "I'm pretty sure she will. Stay here, and I'll go ask her."

My heart raced as I quickly ran back to my seat and waited for Ms. Del Toro to walk in. I had another chance to make it work with Zeb and Monta. But I had no idea how I would explain myself.

Chapter 56

What Happens Now?

Within seconds, Ms. Del Toro's door opened, but she didn't step into the room. "Ms. Orem, it seems there is someone who wants to see you. I can send him away if you don't want to talk to him. It's your choice."

"Who?" I pretended to be surprised, although we both knew I had heard every word.

"Zeb Jones." Ms. Del Toro raised her eyebrows and gave me an are-you-serious look. "Would you like to speak with him?" Before I could answer, Ms. Del Toro narrowed her eyes and added, "Keep in mind, if you keep running away, you will still be running twenty years from now."

The last statement hit me like a brick.

I was already tired. I didn't even want to think about how tired I'd be twenty years from now. I had to figure out how to make this work. Now. Not later.

I nodded slowly and stood up. It felt strange walking out into the hallway to hear what Zeb had to say. But I would push myself to listen. To really listen. I turned the corner and saw Zeb pacing back and forth. As soon as he saw me, he stopped and ran toward me. He wanted to hug me but dropped his arms as he stood in front of me. "Lilly, we were so worried. When you didn't answer your texts, Monta went home to check on you and saw you were gone. Then she found another damn note." He held up a piece of paper that simply read, *"Thanks for all you've done, Lilly."* I dropped my eyes—it was a lame note. "Monta called me, crying and upset. Again! It's a good thing you never turned off your tracker app, or else I wouldn't have found you so quickly."

"I'm sorry," I said as I kept staring at the tile floor. I hadn't turned off the app. How could I have been so stupid? But the fact was, I was so thankful I had forgotten.

"Sorry?" Zeb reached out and lifted my chin. "Lilly, why? What have we done?"

Zeb dropped his hand as I dared to really look at his face. His pale skin was blotchy, and his eyes were red and still teary. Had he been crying over me? "Nothing," I answered truthfully. "It was just too good to be true."

Zeb frowned. "What? So, you would prefer for us to ignore you and not feed you?"

He was so right. It didn't make sense, but I had to step up and be willing to stand there and argue my case. "No, I'm afraid it will be over and not have been real at all."

"So, you ended it before that could happen?" Zeb stated, finally understanding me.

I nodded and swallowed, trying not to cry. "It doesn't make sense. Why do you want me to stay with you? I've done nothing to earn it."

Zeb looked down. I frowned—it was taking too long. Had I upset him? He finally looked up and took a deep breath. "We had three miscarriages before Zonta and thought we were going to lose her too. Monta had to be on bed rest for four months before Zonta was born. We were so thankful, and we wondered if we should try to have another baby. But we never did—there had already been too much loss."

"I'm sorry," was all I could say, feeling guilty for pushing the issue.

But Zeb wasn't finished. "We never made a big deal of not having more children and always told Zonta she was our miracle baby. So, when you came along, it was just too easy—too perfect. Suddenly, we had another kid. Then, suddenly, we didn't. Twice. We shouldn't have put that level of expectation on you. It wasn't fair to you. I'm so sorry. Maybe we should have said something when you moved back in, and then none of this—"

"Are you serious?" My mouth hung open. "Are you really apologizing to me?" This was not charity.

Zeb nodded, "I don't know what else to say." He turned to Ms. Del Toro, who was standing behind me. "What happens to her now?"

"That's Ms. Orem's call. Not mine." Her voice sounded calm and at peace. She trusted that I would do what was right—what was best for me.

Zeb looked back at me and held out his hand, palm up. "Lilly, I tried to come after you last January, but the police wouldn't let me bring you home. They said that you didn't want me to come get you. Please let me take you home this time. Please."

Home. I looked at his hand, and it was shaking just a little. This man and his wife cared so much about me that they were torn apart. I had hurt them twice, and they still came after me. The truth? They really wanted me in their lives. I finally understood why. It was real. And, somehow, I'd have to learn to trust what was real.

I reached out my hand and placed it in his. His eyes grew wide, and he pulled me into his arms and hugged me as he sobbed. I sobbed, too, as I said, "I'm sorry," over and over again.

He pulled away from me and looked down at me. "Promise me, no more goodbye notes. Ever!"

I laughed and sobbed at the same time. "I promise."

I meant it.

Chapter 57

Home

My entire trip to Ruth's Place and back happened before Zonta came home from school. She walked through the door with my make-up work and a big smile on her face like nothing had happened. It didn't take long for her to realize that both Zeb and Monta were home early from work. They were having a deep discussion with me in their living room. Our living room.

We all filled Zonta in on what had happened. Then we all agreed what it would look like moving forward as a family. Family. Strange word. It would take time to get used to, but I had time.

When we were done talking, Zeb took us out to eat to celebrate our family. All four of us. I was okay with his over-the-top idea—he was doing it to show me he cared.

For the first time, I could see Zeb and Monta as adults that I could learn to trust. I could finally see that any rules they had as a family were just a way of life, not a way to keep me from being in charge of my own life. That was a huge step for me, although it would take time for me to really believe it was real. I was thankful that I already trusted Zonta—she'd help me with anything that might still cause any doubt.

I went to work that evening and felt relief that I hadn't chosen to leave June working short again.

I was thankful the week unfolded with no more crisis. No longer a need to run. All my clothes were in the bedroom closet, the empty suitcase tucked away in the corner. My green camo backpack only carried the items I needed for school.

Sometimes, my inner voice said that it was too good to be true. But I fought it with the truth. I reminded myself that everything was real. There would be times that it might not be perfect or that we would have arguments, but that was normal. That was the way families acted and grew closer. I almost looked forward to those moments. If what Ms. Del Toro said was true, then that would be one way for me to prove to Zeb and Monta *and* myself that I did trust them.

Ms. Del Toro had signed me up for a program to help me set up my bank account. But it was no longer because I was planning on taking off and living in my own place that summer. I'd simply have a safe place to save my money for when I needed it—in the future. Right now, I had a chance to live with people who wanted me there. They had no expectations except to talk things through.

That week, I joined Ozzie, Emma, Blake, and Zonta at lunch. It was fun when Mateo decided to join us—a huge sign that he had found his friend group too!

We were a strange bunch, each with our own stories. Each so different. We saw the world through different eyes—still, we were friends because we were learning to trust each other.

Funny really. This past school year, we had been fighting it out as each one of us walked through tough times. Yet, trust grew because we chose to stay in each other's lives. I still had a lot to learn about building healthy friendships. But I quickly understood that was true for everybody.

The reality was we didn't always agree, but we knew one thing for sure. We looked out for each other, and we always had, even before any of us recognized that as friendship.

Chapter 58

Together

Zonta looked beautiful in her red prom dress, standing next to Joseph in our living room. Zeb and Monta took a million pictures of them and even pulled me in for some silly pics, with me and my blue jeans and favorite blue sweater. A cool breeze blew as I stood at the front door with Zeb and Monta. We watched the dressed-up couple hop into Joseph's car and drive off. As soon as they pulled out of the driveway, an old van pulled up. I recognized that van. It was Ozzie in his family's van.

"I think we'll head inside," Monta said as she pulled Zeb back through the front door. "Give you two some privacy."

"What?" I asked. But before they could explain, Zeb closed the door. The last thing I saw was his huge grin. I shook my head at the closed door before I turned around to watch Ozzie climb out of his van.

I was confused as I watched the smiling football all-star walk toward me. His jeans and black T-shirt told me he was not going to push me to go to the prom at the last minute.

I smiled and leaned against the front door. "What are you doing here?"

"I'm going to give you your birthday gift." He grinned as he pulled his cap off his head and held it over his chest. "A date, no questions asked."

"Now?" I laughed. "You aren't planning on doing some weird prom thing with me, like dance in the parking lot as we listen to Mateo and the Bent Rays rock out inside."

Ozzie laughed. "No, but that could have been fun."

"Maybe." I smiled but then quickly asked, "So, where are you taking me?"

"You'll have to wait and see." He shoved his cap back on and started walking toward his van. "Are you coming?"

My stomach flipped, in a good way. I popped my head inside and told Monta that I was headed out with Ozzie, and she told me to have fun but be safe. I smiled and told her I would—there was no way I was looking for anything but safe.

We drove along Bence Avenue and up Seaberg Avenue and then left onto 17th Street. "You better not be taking me to school. Or the football stadium. It's not that great at night, trust me."

"You'll see," Ozzie said as he kept his eyes on the road.

I was relieved when we passed the high school but was surprised when we pulled up to 17th Street Café. I looked at him and frowned. This had been the place where we worked on the project together. The same night I knew that I liked him—the same night I was beat up. "Why are you taking me here?"

Ozzie parked the van and looked over at me. He saw my disappointment but reached over and squeezed my hand. "Trust me."

I did, so I followed him inside. There were only a few people there, which was good since I was already nervous. I didn't need judging eyes from anyone wondering why Ozzie was taking me out. Ozzie took my hand and pulled me to the back corner. The normally cheap café-style table was covered with a small white tablecloth and a vase with a single rose.

"Did you do this yourself?" I asked, feeling my cheeks warm.

"My mother hired 17th Street Café to cater a gig in Newport last month. They were more than happy to do me a favor." He pulled out a chair for me and then sat down across from me, dropping his cap into the seat next to him. A few minutes later, a young guy brought us each a large iced coffee—the same drink Ozzie had that night last fall. The drink that I had asked him if I could finish. I shivered at the memory, but I didn't say anything since the young guy quickly returned with a platter of six different kinds of pastries.

"Wow, this is more than we can eat," I stated, thankful there was more than just the drinks.

"Speak for yourself," he teased.

We tore into the cinnamon rolls—sticky icing all over our fingers. Neither one of us cared. After half the roll was gone, I finally asked, "Why did you bring me here?"

He looked at me, really looked at me. His dark brown eyes were filled with a seriousness that I had never seen before. He grabbed a napkin to wipe off his fingers. "To start over."

I felt a part of me melt away. "Start over?" I followed Ozzie's lead and wiped my fingers clean too.

"I want to erase any bad memory from this place. I want to let tonight unfold like it should have last fall." He reached into his back jeans pocket and pulled out a little tissue paper with something wrapped inside. He pushed the tissue across the table toward me. "You were the only one who always saw me for who I really was, from the beginning." He lifted his hand off the tissue.

I slowly opened it but then froze when my hands touched a beautiful blue ribbon. I looked up at Ozzie, and my heart began to race. I had no words.

He reached his hand across the table and touched the blue ribbon only an inch away from my hand. He smiled gently as my memories came flooding back. When I was little, Granny used to braid my hair and tie the ends with a blue ribbon. She would make me stand in front of her so she could look at me. All of me. And then she would smile and tell me that I was beautiful and that the blue ribbon made my magic shine. I believed her and felt pretty and strong—I felt bulletproof.

I had forgotten that I had told Ozzie about the ribbon and Granny. Had he remembered it all these months?

My heart pounded in my chest as Ozzie lifted his hand over mine. The soft blue ribbon felt like an old friend. Familiar. "Lilly, your granny was right about that magic—you *still* have it. You always have, with or without the ribbon. You have a way of speaking life into me and others. Even if it ticks us off." I laughed out loud but didn't move my hand. His warm touch meant something different to me at that moment.

"Ozzie, I—" I started.

"I'm not finished." He squeezed my hand. "You *are* strong. And we all know you are bulletproof." He smiled and then added, "I want you to remember that. Not only because your granny said it, but because I said it." Then he held my hand tight and asked, "Can we start over from the beginning? Forget how awful I was? Forget it all?"

My heart continued to pound. "Ozzie, no." Before he could react, I quickly added, "I don't ever want to forget it. It has made us who we are today. There is nothing to be ashamed of, for either one of us." I wrapped my other hand over Ozzie's hand. "But I am ready to move forward. Together."

Acknowledgments

Writing Lilly could never have happened without the help of several individuals. I am forever grateful to each of you for the time and support you provided.

To my parents Jonlyn and G. Keith Parker, who were willing to take on the first read-through of the manuscript. They have not only embraced the characters' lives with gusto, but they have shown unwavering support for the whole writing process. To Ben Onachila, who was also willing to take on the first read-through and provide me with refreshing feedback. His uncanny poetic ability has helped me iron out some rough edges. To Kym Sebranek, Sheila Mooney, Michael Bower, and Dr. Tara P. Bacote for reading through the manuscript and providing valuable feedback, each bringing their unique perspective to the table, supporting my desire to provide an authentic story. To Nastia Parker for guiding me through the intricate world of social media and texting trends.

Thanks to Barbara Grimm and Olivia Shuler for their insight into teen homelessness and Emily Lowery and Teresa Adkins for insight into homelessness and running a homeless shelter. Also, a special thanks to Emily Lowery for reading through the manuscript, willing to validate the authenticity of Lilly's journey.

Thanks to Renee Roof, not only for insight into the plight of teen homelessness and the foster care system and the realities of DSS involvement, but also her willingness to read through the manuscript to confirm the authenticity of the details as they unfold within *Lilly*.

To my daughters, Sarah Borhaug and Maya Borhaug, whose read-throughs helped me keep the story real. Sarah's commitment, creativity, and professional skill in editing and designing the cover are also deeply appreciated as well as her willingness to model for the cover. Maya's willingness to continue genuine dialogue over authentic character growth and plot development added a level of professional depth to the story that is deeply appreciated.

To my daughter, Amy Borhaug, who whispers words of perseverance and courage, and Nioca Robinson, who provided valuable insight woven into Mrs. Wilkes's character and whose encouragement and friendship I dearly value.

To my copy editor Julie Overpeck, who not only understands the importance of Hi-Lo books but helped turn out a professional product.

A special thanks to Transylvania County Schools and Brevard High School for the use of their property for the cover shot.

Last but not least, thank you to my husband, Tore, for his insight into building trust among the unhoused and his unwavering support and his steady grounding. Without him, none of it would be possible.

Lilly's Text/Slang/Terms

The following are definitions of terms, including texting and slang, used in *Lilly*. Some terms may also have other definitions that are not included in this mini-glossary.

@—at

2—to, too, two

4—four, for

accept at face value—to take something as it is and not add a deeper meaning that is not or may not be there

abandoned/sense of abandonment—to completely give up on someone or something. *A sense of abandonment* is the feeling that one has been completely left alone or given up on.

abt—about

bus tables—clear tables

charity—help/aid given to those in need

couch surfing—to sleep in different homes and places other than one's own home

deer-in-the-headlights look—to look lost, confused

Department of Social Services (DSS)—state and federal government program that provides help for families in poverty, deals with domestic violence issues, and offers many other services to people in need.

dozen—12

flip on its head—to turn upside down

frosted window—when the glass on a window is covered with a white substance so it is not see-through

gn—goodnight

going through the motions—play along, to say or do what one needs to be said or done but not mean it

the hand you were dealt—what you have. Often, it means that one has limits because of the situation they are in and can do nothing else about it.

legally binding—something (in this case, it is a contract) that can be enforced by the law if it is not followed

lol—laugh out loud

makeshift—something that is made or put together for a short period of time and is not meant to last long

omg—oh my gosh/God/goodness

plz—please

read between the lines—to understand the meaning when it is not directly stated

ring a bell—sound familiar; when something brings back a memory or a thought that causes something to make sense

rmbr—remember

rope into something—make someone do something they do not want to do

safety assessment plan—a close look at someone's living situation (or workplace) to see if there is anything that might be harmful. If anything is found to be a problem, then a plan is put in place to make sure the space becomes and stays safe.

shooed off—chased away

sux—sucks

takes guts—must be brave to do something; courage

talk trash—to say bad things about a person. This can happen in front of that person or when they are not around to hear.

to stand on your own two feet—be able to rely or depend on yourself

trespassing—to illegally be on someone else's property

ttyl—talk to you later

ur—you're/your

w—with

y—why

www.ingramcontent.com/pod-product-compliance
Lightning Source LLC
Chambersburg PA
CBHW030934210726
48290CB00007B/2189